Lock Down Publications and Ca$h
Presents

I0664787

IF YOU CROSS
ME ONCE 6

COFFINS AND CONSEQUENCES

Written By

Anthony Fields

First Edition 2025

Printed in the United States of America

This is a work of fiction. Names, characters, places, and incidents either are products of the author's imagination or are used fictitiously. Any similarity to actual events or locales or persons, living or dead, is entirely coincidental.

Lock Down Publications
P.O. Box 944
Stockbridge, GA 30281
www.lockdownpublications.com

Like our page on Facebook: Lock Down Publications
www.facebook.com/lockdownpublications.ldp

Stay Connected with Us!

Text **LOCKDOWN** to 22828 to stay up-to-date with new
releases, sneak peaks, contests and more…

Like our page on Facebook:
Lock Down Publications

Join Lock Down Publications/The New Era Reading Group

Visit our website:
www.lockdownpublications.com

Follow us on Instagram:
Lock Down Publications

Email Us: We want to hear from you!

DEDICATION

THIS ONE IS DEDICATED TO ALL THE PEOPLE WHO RECOGNIZE A SICK PEN GAME. THIS IS ALSO DEDICATED TO KENNETH HOFFMAN AND ERRON ROBINSON.

SALUTE.

CHAPTER 1

REN TYLER

"What the fuck is going on, Ron?" Dorenda Tyler asked as soon as she walked in through the door of the apartment. "And who is this?"

"This is Bionca, Ma. She's Brion's sister and a good friend of mine."

"That answers the second question. What about the first one?"

I thought about exactly what I wanted to tell my mother and instantly decided to tell her everything about everything. She could be trusted. "This all started when Brion's brother Byron got killed…"

"Wait," my mother said, "this seems like it's gonna take a while, so let me get out of these wet clothes and this coat and shit. And I need a drink. What do you got in here to drink?"

"White liquor and brown liquor. Your favorite, Ma. They're in the kitchen. In the cabinet over the refrigerator."

Dorenda Tyler pulled off her coat and hat. "Good. Get me some yoga pants and a long sleeve—no, it's kinda warm in here, get me a T-shirt to put on. And some dry socks." As I turned to get the clothes my mother requested, I could hear my mother say, "Sorry to hear about your brothers, Bionca."

Minutes later, I returned to the living room. I waited until after she had changed into the clothes before continuing my story. "After Brion's brother got killed, it fucked him up bad. He loved his brother to death. He wanted revenge. After a brief street investigation, we learned... he learned that a dude named Sean Branch killed his brother—"

"Teflon Sean." My mother said after sipping the liquor in her cup.

"You know him?" Bionca asked immediately.

My mother shook her head and shifted her position in the recliner. "Didn't know—well, don't know him personally. Heard about him a lot over the years before he went to jail back in the day. Ren's father spoke about him all the time. Sean was a teenager back then, but Von respected his reputation for killing grown men who were labeled hard to kill. Sean was a protege of a man named Ameen Bashir. Ameen Bashir was another vicious killer that was well known all over the city. He and Von were friends. They'd come up together in a juvenile jail called Maple Glen which later became Cedar Knoll. Von thought highly of the man and teen. As the years went on and Ameen Bashir was killed, it seemed like Sean Branch became a killing machine. No murder charge could stick to him, thus him being labeled Teflon Sean. The streets didn't give him that nickname. The local media did."

"Well, Ma, that killing machine came home and he's still killing. Allegedly, he took some money to kill Byron—"

"My big brother." Bionca added.

"The streets is saying that Byron... street name Crud, is supposed to have told on some dudes from MLK Avenue. Buck or somebody, Lacy somebody or something. Something about a drug conspiracy case. Sean is supposed to have—"

"Not supposed to have. He did kill Crud."

"Please, Bionca, let me tell the story. Anyway, Ma, Sean killed Bionca's brother and cut his head off—"

"On Third Street Southeast, a month or so ago. I saw that on the news. The house was set on fire, but it didn't burn all the way." My mother said.

"Yes, Ma, but if you don't mind, just like I just told Bionca, can I please just get the story out?" My mother nodded. "Okay. Once Brion learned that Sean Branch—— hold on a minute… wait. What was that you just said earlier? The name you mentioned as Sean Branch's mentor?"

My mother stopped sipping on her liquor and looked up at me quizzically. "Who? Ameen Bashir?"

I turned to face Bionca. Something in my mind clicked. "The dude Quran that was with Sean when he killed Crud, what's his name again? His whole name. You said it to me before."

Bionca livened up suddenly. "Quan Bashir. His last name is Bashir. Tosheka said him and his brothers are all Bashirs."

"So, you think that guy…Quran is some kin to Ameen?" My mother asked.

"Gotta be. Given the fact that he's Sean's sidekick now. Must be Ameen Bashir's nephew, cousin or son. Ma, do you know anything about Ameen Bashir?"

"Other than the fact that he's dead? Uh… I knew that he was from Southeast. Over by Barry farms, I think." My mother shrugged her shoulders. "That's it. Oh… and he was rumored to be really gorgeous. Brown skinned with dark curly hair and light grey eyes."

"Light grey eyes!" Bionca exclaimed and stood up." They're related. You just described Quran. To the letter. Tosheka bragged about that man every time I talked to her. And the crazy part is… she used all the same words you just did."

"Okay… wait," my mother said. "I'm lost. What does Ameen Bashir's… relative have to do with this? With my fuckin' house blowing up and my nephew getting killed?"

Bionca, sit back down. You're distracting me." Once Bionca had retaken her seat on the couch across from my mother, I began talking. "Sean killed Crud and the dude Quan killed a dude named Whistle, one of Crud's friends. Word is that they both told on the same conspiracy case. There was another dude present at the house on Third Street. A dude named Doo Doo. He threw the alley oop for Sean to get Crud. Brion knew who Doo Doo was and where he hung out. Hold up... I skipped a part. Me and Brion went to Orleans Place to see a guy. Guy named Miguel. He was a friend of Crud's too. The day we went to see Miguel, him and Brion exchanged some heated words and Miguel threatened Brion. That pissed him off—"

"And you killed him for threatening Brion?" My mother asked.

I nodded.

"The apple don't fall far from the tree. Finish the story."

"I killed two people that day. Miguel and some other dude that was with him. A third dud got shot but he survived. After that we went to see Doo Doo on Langston Lane. We took him to Half Street down Southwest and Brion interrogated him. He came clean about throwing the alley-oop. I killed him. Brion took his cellphone and found a number stored in the phone for Sean Bashir. He sent Sean a text message asking to meet up. It worked. We went to Naylor Road to ambush Sean and he saw through our ruse. Me and Brion opened fire on Sean's car, but he got away unscathed—"

"Not before peeping who it was who was trying to ambush him." Bionca interjected. "And this is the part of the story that hurts me the most. Brion came to me and told me that it was Sean Branch, who killed Crud and cut his head off. I remember that night like it was yesterday."

"I was sitting at the dining room table putting a picture collage together for Crud's memorial when Brion walked into the house.

"You up late." Brion said. "As usual."

"You know me. Last to sleep, first one to rise. What brings you here this late?"

Brion didn't answer. He just grabbed a chair and positioned it next to me. His eyes on the collage I was assembling.

"For the memorial, there will be a large poster-like picture of Byron sitting on a… whatever that thing is called. There will be obituaries with photos. A lot of photos. A couple of people will speak. Mommy, of course. Me, Brechelle, you if you want to. Other than family and friends. There will be a few songs sung, some poems read. That's about it. Then we'll find a place for a repast. Mommy hadn't picked a date for the memorial, but Brion's being cremated at the crematorium out in Brandywine, Maryland next week. So, again what brings you here this late."

"I found out who killed Crud. But first, let me tell you what's happened since we last talked. I got a good man that I fuck with from Morris Road named Baby Gas. Him and his men hang on MLK and Talbert Street. The dudes that went to jail from down there eight niggas. An oldhead named James 'Dr. L' Venable, Daryl 'Dee' Smithe, the dude Lacy who also hung Uptown and in Stanton Oaks, Buckey Fields, Lonnell 'L' Tucker, some nigga named Foots from Congress Park, Caliwoo and Whistle—"

"Whistle? Crud's man Whistle?"

Brion nodded. "Yeah, but he ran the people while the others took cops or went to trial. Here's where things got sketchy. According to my man, five of the eight went to trial and Crud ended up being the only witness to testify against them—"

"But what does Crud have to do with a conspiracy case dealing with niggas on MLK Avenue in a barbershop? He never hung down there, did he?"

"Not that I know of, but according to my man and street talk, Crud got locked up for armed robbery—"

"I remember that. He was at D.C. jail for a minute."

"I remember that too. While he was there, he was in one of the housing units with the dude Buckey Fields. Crud allegedly let the dude Buckey Fields see his discovery in the armed robbery case. The dude saw a statement that Crud had made saying that Whistle was the one who robbed the dude and not him. The dude Buckey Fields confronted Crud about the statement. The way the story goes… Crud checked into Protective Custody that night and later jumped on the barbershop case as a witness, saying that he bought drugs from the dude Buckey Fields off and on for a year. He also testified against the other dudes too.

"Miguel said that Crud had told on the dude Lacy… and that he put up the money, but may now says different. He said that the dude Buckey Fields put up the money on Crud's head. Aight, with that said, that brings me to Doo Doo. I talked to Doo Doo. He denied having a hand in Crud's murder. After a little persuasion, he talked. The person that killed Crud is a dude named Sean Branch. He killed Crud and cut off his head. Whistle was killed by a dud that was with Sean. According to Doo Doo and confirmed by what Miguel said before, Whistle made statements on that same case. The dude Buckey Fields was a friend of Whistle's. He was on the run during the trial, but he got picked up later.

"Whistle copped out to some short shit but not before making the statements implicating the others on the case. The dude with Sean Branch recognized Whistle's name and killed him after Sean killed Crud. Doo Doo threw the oops and gave Crud to Sean Branch. I took Doo Doo's phone and found a number for Sean Branch. I sent him a text. The nigga went for the flim flam, but had God on his side. Me and Ren tried to cook his ass on Nayler Road, but he got away. End of story."

"Sean Branch, huh?"

"Yeah," Brion replied. "You hip to him?"

"I'm hip to Sean Branch, Brion. Damn near the whole city is hip to him. He's bad news. Dangerous. Vicious. Just came home some months ago, I think. I saw it all over the news. Back in the day, he killed so many people and got away with it, that he earned the nickname Teflon Sean. No murder charges were ever brought up on him. No crime could stick to him. But he ended up getting charged for a murder that he didn't commit and somehow he got found guilty for it. That was almost eighteen years ago. He gotta be like thirty nine or forty now. Looks Hispanic with dark curly hair."

"That's him. He's grown a beard now."

"The game just got super serious, baby brother. You tried to kill Sean Branch and didn't. You said he looked at you, right?"

"Yeah, he looked right at me and Ren, then he ducked low and got out of there. We put over twenty rounds or better in his car. A Porsche with paper tags on it. Still can't figure out how he figured out that we was gonna hit him."

"Sean Branch is a different kind of killer. He's rumored to have been killing since he was eleven or twelve. Maybe younger. He saw your face, so he knows what you look like and that ain't good. Now it all makes sense. Cutting off Brion's head was critical to getting the message out. Sean wants the streets to know that he's back, and he's even more cold hearted than before. You have to find him, Brion. And find him soon—"

"My brother was unprepared to hunt a dud like Sean Branch and I knew that. I let my grief and ego get the best of me. I sent Brion to his death—"

"Bionca, stop it." We already talked about this—"

"You and I talked about it, Ren. Not me and your mother. If we gon' tell her everything, we tell her everything. I should have never told Brion to go after Sean Branch. I should have told him to stand down until we could figure some shit out. I am responsible for his death and had you never went to the bathroom in Stewart's, I'd be responsible for your death, too."

"Ren," my mother said, "what is she talking about?"

I took a moment to gather my wits. "I'm pregnant, Ma. I found out that day Brion was killed. After the memorial service, I felt sick. I'd been feeling sick a lot before that day. Having been pregnant before, I recognized the symptoms that I was having. I bought a home pregnancy test the morning of the memorial, but I never got around to using it, until I was at the funeral home. When me and Brion were leaving the funeral home, I needed to use the bathroom. While in there, I decided to pee on the applicator for the test. I told Brion to go ahead to the car and that I'd be there in a minute. He left without me... and... and—" Tears formed in my eyes and fell.

My mother rose from the recliner to comfort me.

"I'm good, Ma." I said and stopped her in her tracks. "Really, I'm good." I wiped at the tears in my eyes and the ones that stained my cheeks.

Sean Branch killed Brion and he would have killed me had I been with him."

My mother sat her now empty glass on the table near her. "How do you know that it was Sean Branch who did it? Did somebody see him there?"

"Nobody saw him there, Mrs. Tyler, but we are sure that it was him. There is no other explanation for it." Bionca said.

"I hear you, but how could you be so sure? Maybe someone close to Miguel figured out that Brion had something to do with the murders on Orleans Place. Maybe it was someone else. Maybe Brion was killed for a different reason."

"Ma, it was him. Sean Branch killed Brion. In my heart, I know it's true. So, I acted on it. I went online and found out about Sean's daughter. Shontay. She was twenty years old. She worked at the Chipotle at Galaxy Place. I went to her job and followed her to her car. Then, I killed her."

"Are you serious?" my mother asked. "You killed Sean Branch's daughter?"

"Yep. And wanted to kill his mother, but I didn't get to. Sean's mother committed suicide when she learned about her granddaughter's murder. I assume that Sean Branch now knows that I did it. That I killed his daughter. And he knows something about Bionca, too. How do I know that? Because it was Sean Branch who went to Bionca's house on Southern Avenue and killed a woman named Celine... a friend of Bionca's, thinking that she was Bionca."

"He was there waiting for me to come home. I couldn't go inside the house. It held too many bad memories. Celine decided to go in the house and get some things I needed. It was raining. She put on my hat and walked to the house. He appeared out of nowhere and gunned Celine down on the front porch. Afterwards, he walked away."

"Again," my mother stated empathetically, "did you see him? Are you sure that the killer was Sean Branch?"

"And again," I said with equal conviction. "I'm telling you it was him. It was Sean Branch. Then after killing Celine, he went to your house and made it explode. He killed Dame as he ran out of the house. All of that was him, Ma. Sean Branch did everything I just said. All of it. I'm sure of it."

"So just to be clear, Sean Branch killed my nephew Damien and he's looking for you and Bionca?"

Me and Bionca both nodded our heads at the same time.

"And Ameen Bashir's relative, probably his son has what to do with this?"

"Nothing really, other than he was with Sean when he killed Byron." Bionca replied. "We just decided that if we can find Quran... we might can find Sean."

"Find Sean and then what?" My mother asked.

"Kill his ass!" Bionca and I both said simultaneously.

"If what you say is true and y'all truly believe that Sean Branch is the person who blew my house up and killed my nephew, then your duo just became a trio."

I looked at Dorenda Tyler with a confused look. "A trio? And what exactly does that mean, Ma?"

My mother stood up, walked to the kitchen and filled her glass with Patron. She walked back to the recliner and sat down. "I have a confession to make, Ren. Earlier when you told me about you killing the dudes on Orleans Place and I said that the apple didn't fall far from the tree. I wasn't talking about your father's tree. I was talking about my tree. Your father wasn't the only killer in the family. He taught me to kill way before her taught you. And I learned my lessons well. When the boy next door raped you and got you pregnant—"

"I killed him the next day and days later, Dad killed—" My mother shook her head. "No. Days later I killed that boy's mother and grandmother. Your father only killed the dogs. The pit bulls. That's my confession to you. Our neighbors weren't the only people I killed, Ren. After your father's death, I killed everybody who I thought might've killed Von. Everybody. So, now I'm about to become the old me. My daughter's life and her unborn child's life is in danger. I just lost my house and my favorite nephew, so I'm involved now. If you and Bionca want to catch Sean Branch and kill him, count me in. But we gotta be careful.

"With my name involved, that ups the stakes. I have never been arrested for any murder, but I've been the suspect in a lot of them. I've been questioned and interrogated, but I know how to play the game. Just like I did the other day when the detective investigating Dame's murder questioned me. I played the grieving, innocent aunt and I think the detective went for it. I don't know. I don't care. I'm in. We are all in this together. For Brion, for y'all and for Dame."

CHAPTER 2

BIONCA CLARK

I could hear Ren's mother's loud snores from the next room. Ren stood in the doorway of her bedroom, eyes on the sleeping form on her couch.

"Damn," Ren said, "I wonder when was the last time my mother got some sleep. She knocked out, snoring like shit. I ain't never heard her sound like that. Woman sound like a fuckin' grizzly bear out there. Maybe it was the alcohol. With her crazy ass. All this time, I thought my father was the cold blooded psycho in the family, today I find out it was her ass the whole time. If my father—"

I walked up behind Ren and covered her mouth with my hand. With my other hand, I pulled her out of the doorway. Using my face, I moved her hair so that I could get to the side of her neck. My tongue touched her skin and took on a life of its own. My tongue found Ren's ear and licked it. My nostrils became full of her scent. Her hair smelled of fruity shampoo, her body a different elixir. A more natural, heady scent that aroused me heavily. My left hand walked slowly down Ren's body until it found the waistband of her sweat pants. Ren tried to wiggle out of my embrace but I held her there. Soft protestations tried to escape her mouth, but my hand that still covered her mouth muffled those. I moved my hand deeper into her sweat pants until they were inside her panties.

Undeterred, I grazed over the shaved area where hair was starting to grow. Then my fingers journeyed on. Ren's pussy was soaking wet. Her juices coated my fingers instantly. Quickly, I pulled my hand out of her sweat pants and licked each finger. Her pussy tasted so good. I put my hand back inside Ren's panties and began to alternate between gently rubbing her clit and penetrating her wetness. Ren's body responded to my touch. My fingers, lips and tongue were too aggressive to deny. I could feel Ren's breath on my fingers. I could hear her soft moans that couldn't escape fingers. I stopped moving momentarily to listen for the sounds of her mother's snores reverberating loudly in the next room.

The snores were there. Still strong and unrelenting. Knowing that Ren had never experienced a woman before me made me bold. I thought about the conversation we'd had last night after I kissed her and then seduced her.

"I never—" Ren started.

"Don't talk Ren. Let's just savor the moment." I told her.

"That's the problem. I am savoring the moment and it feels wrong."

"I disagree. It feels right to me."

"It feels like I just cheated on Blast."

"You're overthinking it, Ren."

"Shit feel like incest."

"Incest? Stop what you're doing, Ren. We are not related."

"But, I've always looked at you, thought of you as a sister."

"I'm not your sister, Ren. You were fucking my brother."

"I know that part... I'm just saying. That shit felt so good just now, but it can never happen again, Bionca."

"Okay, Ren."

"I'm serious, Bionca. Promise me that you will respect my decision."

"I promise."

Ren's body gyrated onto my fingers. I couldn't see her eyes, but I knew that they were closed. Just as they had been last night when the feelings she couldn't control overtook her. If I had a disk, this would be the point where I'd take it out and stroke it. Removing my hand from inside Ren's panties, I first put my hand inside my own panties while I continued to assault Ren's neck with kisses and licks. My own orgasm called out for attention. For a need to come down. I was so aroused that it didn't take me long to find eruption. Fingers still wet with my own wetness, I used them to yank at Ren's sweats. I eased her sweat pants down to her ankles. Obediently, Ren stepped out of each pants leg on her own. I could still hear the sounds of Dorenda Tyler's loud snores. Inside, I smiled. The hand that had been covering Ren's mouth was now removed.

"Bionca... stop!" Ren protested as I turned her around. I ignored Ren. I needed to taste her pussy. I needed to make her cum several times and taste each one.

"You promised!"

I was on my knees by then. One of Ren's legs was on my shoulder. My face was in between her legs and my tongue was inside her pussy. Slowly, I lapped at her middle like a kitten with a bowl of milk.

"Stop, Bionca...stop! You promised!"

***

"Ma, what about work?" Ren asked her mother as we sat at the table in the dining room eating crab and shrimp.

"What about it?" Dorenda Tyler replied. "I can't work and look for Sean Branch. I got vacation time and an extra leave that I never took. I'ma be good. Besides, getting Sean Branch in the ground has become priority number one."

"We can't go to any funerals or anything like that for nobody." Ren said and looked from her mother to me. "That goes for Celine and Dame. Sean knows how to find funerals and memorials. He'll expect us to attend those things."

"I agree," I said. Which brings me to another thought. Sean was able to find out where Crud's memorial was. He found my mother's house on Southern Avenue. He found out that you… Ren, was the woman with Brion when y'all tried to kill him. That took him to your mother's house in Ivy city. So, my questions are how in the hell does Sean Branch process information so fast? And does he have help?"

"Good point, Bionca. Let me go back and try to see if we are missing something. Okay, Sean Branch kills Byran and cuts off his head. He thinks it stops there. Brion and I investigate and learn that Doo Doo is involved. Doo Doo admits his involvement and tell us that Sean Branch killed Byron. Me and Brion attempt to ambush and kill Sean Branch. He sees us and gets away unscathed. Sean must've immediately went after Doo Doo's phone on which we sent the text. I'm guessing that somebody on Langston Lane must've told Sean about Brion picking Doo Doo up..."

"That's assuming that somebody on the Lane recognized Brion," Dorenda added.

"Either that or Sean somehow put two and two together and came up with my brother."

"Well, we know that he did. Sean does his due diligence and finds out that your family is holding a memorial for Crud. He goes there and sees Brion. He killed my baby. After that Mama Clark passes away. You and I figure that the person who killed Brion was Sean Branch. We find his daughter and I kill her. Sean's mother commits suicide upon learning that her grandbaby is dead. The question becomes, How did Sean connect US to his daughter's death? Because as far as we know, he reacted by looking for US. You and Me, Bionca. And I can't understand how he made that connection so fast."

I dipped a grilled shrimp into sauce before answering. "I'm as confused as you. But we do know two things for sure. SOMEBODY, on the same day, went to my house and killed Celine on the front porch. Then SOMEBODY went to Ivy City..."

"To my fuckin' house and caused it to explode. When my nephew tried to escape the explosion and subsequent fire, he was gunned down as he exited the house," Dorenda Tyler interjected.

"Right," I continued, "and the only person we can come up with is Sean Branch. So, since we only have him, we gotta ask ourselves the obvious questions. Finding out where I live isn't rocket science. There is any number of ways Sean could get my address. But how did he come up with Ren's? And better yet, if he came up with your mother's address, how do we know that he won't come up with this one? This condo is in your name Ren. As far as we know Sean Branch would be in the hallway as we speak or outside in the parking lot." I looked at Ren who looked at her mother, who looked back at me. The next thing that happened, happened in a blur. We moved with alacrity. In seconds, a gun was in each of our hands.

"Ma," Ren said and smiled. "You still carrying that same gun?"

Dorrenda Tyler led the way to the condo door. "Haven't failed me yet. Let's go. We checking the hallway, the building... does this building have a back door?"

Ren nodded. "The back exit is on the bottom floor. One level below the front entrance."

"Good. I'ma take the front exit. Just walk right out the door into the parking lot. I assume if Sean knows where my house is and who my family is, he also knows what I look like. Assuming he does and he's out there, he won't expect me to be strapped. You two are the key, though. He won't be suspecting the three of us to be looking for him. You come up around the building and look for him. One of y'all spot him, holla out and we all box him in. Does that make sense to y'all?"

Me and Ren both nodded our heads.

Dorenda Tyler laughed suddenly." Would you two bitched please go put shoes and shit on. Y'all nodding y'all heads, eyes big as paper plates and y'all got flip flops and shit on. Go get dressed and let's do this. I hope his ass is outside so that I can kill his ass, Go!"

"A woman was killed on the Clark family's front porch..."

"Celine James. Saw it on the news. I killed her. Thought she was Bionca Clark."

"Bionca Clark is still alive as far as we know although her whereabouts are unknown. If you find her and decide to kill her, be discreet. I understand that discretion is not your forte, but do it. And I mean discreet as in whatever you did with Stephan Hartwell, Maurice Brooks and a few others who remain on a missing person list. That means no more hand grenades. That creates too much fear in law enforcement circles. And no more cutting off people's heads. Draws too much attention and the local news will latch on to shit like that and never let go. Lastly, are you familiar with a man named Von Tyler? He's dead now, but he was notorious..."

"Killer back in the day. I'm hip to Von Tyler. Why do you ask?"

"Because in most cases the fruit never falls far from the tree. But you already know that given the fact that you are definitely Bruno Branch's son. Anyway, Von Tyler has a daughter—"

"Renaissance Tyler. I'm hip to her, too."

"Good, so you already know, huh?" Detective Bob Mathis asked. Confusion etched across my face. "Already know what? That Von Tyler has a daughter?'

"Naw, not that. Since you know who she is, I'm figuring that you know that she was Brion Clark's girlfriend."

"I did not know that. But what..."

"What does she have to do with this conversation at this moment? Let me tell you. Renaissance Tyler drives a burgundy Infiniti SUV and the video footage from outside the Chipotle on the night that Shontay was killed shows a dark colored Infiniti SUV parked outside for about an hour or so. The video shows Shantay exit the Chipotle at 12:05 a.m. At 12:06 a.m., a woman exits the driver's side of the Infiniti and follows Shantay. Minutes later that same woman runs back to the Infiniti SUV, enters it and pulls off. I believe that woman was Renaissance Tyler. She's the person who killed your daughter."

My phone vibrating against the surface of the truck's center console, broke my reverie. By the time I grabbed the phone it ceased to vibrate. The call had ended, but momentarily a text message came through…

"On my way. Will be there in five minutes."

Sitting the phone back down, I let myself go back to the conversation I'd had with Bob Mathis early this morning.

"Are you one hundred percent sure that the woman was Renaissance Tyler?

"One hundred percent? No. About ninety five percent sure, yes. Her motive is clear. She's pissed that you killed her boyfriend. Somehow she found out about your daughter. Social media probably led her straight to Chipotle's front door." I laughed a low maniacal laugh and dropped one tear, *"Ain't that a bitch. I been looking for Renaissance Tyler for days. Shantay helped me find her on social media. He and the Clark family. All the while, this bitch been looking for me."* I laughed out loud. *"What the fuck? Ren Tyler killed my daughter because she couldn't find me. I blew up her mother's house and killed her cousin because I couldn't find her. That's crazy as shit!"* I laughed hysterically for a long time.

"Sean, you're scaring me, buddy. Straight up. Have you slept any?"

21

*"Sleep is the cousin of death. I'll sleep when I'm dead.
Brion Clark tried to kill me—"*

"What? When?"

I nodded. *"A couple days before I stepped on his ass. Him
and Renaissance Tyler. They killed Doo Doo and used his
phone to send me a text. Told me to meet him on Naylor Road
by Naylor Gardens near Altimont Street. I went there like a
dumb ass without suspecting shit. But when I got there I
instantly noticed that something wasn't right. Doo Doo
would have been there somewhere when I pulled up and he
wasn't. I spotted Brion and a bitch with red hair walking
towards the car. I saw them both reach. My first instinct was
to get low and I did. Then the shots came next—"*

"The cousin's name was Damien Tyler."

*"I know the cousin is the lucky one. He's already dead.
What I'm about to do to the rest of the Tyler's gon' be epic."*

*"Epic? Sean, I just told you about those stupid ass hand
grenades. You can't keep using them—"*

*"I need a copy of that video footage. Can you get that for
me?"*

"Don't see no reason why not. What else do you need?"

*"Can you get the recordings of Quron's brother in his cell
talking?"*

*"Absolutely not. Gamble ain't coming up off of those.
Fairy won't even admit that the recordings are from a bug in
Jihad Bashir's cell. Nobody has a copy of these recordings
but him."*

*"Damn... a'ight, I'll just have to remember everything
you said was on it. I need you to try and get in touch with
Renaissance's mother—"*

"Dorenda Tyler. For what though?"

*"So that I can use her to find her daughter. Then I'ma kill
both of their asses real slow. See if you can set up some type
of meeting with Dorenda Tyler. Use the house exploding and
her nephew getting killed... the whole investigation thing. If
you get her to agree to a meet, you just text me the info and*

let me take it from there. Also, see check your system and see if you can find me any other Tyler's related to Renaissance and Dorenda. Damien's mother and father for instance for some reason, I don't think Renaissance lived at the house on Decator Street. Run her info and see if you can get an address for her. Then try the DMV system. I need all of that and whatever you can find on Bionca and Brechelle Clark. People trust cops. See what you can get for me. ASAP."

"And if I do all of that, then I assume that the surviving Best family members get to keep surviving?

"For now."

The cellphone pinged to alert me to an incoming text message. I looked at the phone.

"I'm here. Where are you?"

Having watched the black Hyundai Genesis pull into the underground parking garage of the Harris Teeter's in Crystal City, I knew that Quran was driving it. I exited the Toyota Tundra and skulked over to the Genesis. Tapping on the window on the passenger side, the door unlocked and I climbed inside. Quran was dressed in similar clothes. All black attire, a thick Hugo Boss beanie pulled low onto his head.

"Assalaam Alaikum," Quran greeted me.

I didn't return the greeting.

"Assalaam Alakum, ocki!" Quran said again.

"I meant what I said the last time we spoke, youngin. Don't make me repeat myself about who and what I am."

"The rope of Allah is—"

"The rope that I'ma use to strangle my enemies with before I kill them. I didn't call you here to talk about me. I called you here to talk about your brother."

The look on Quran's face changed to confusion and anger. "My brother. What about my brother?"

"Get word to your brother and tell him to shut the fuck up in that cell and any other cell—"

"What? Big Homie, you throwin' me the fuck off. What the fuck is you talking about?"

I had to quiet the animal inside me and remind myself that Quran wasn't my enemy. "Greg Gamble has your brother's cell bugged. I got a reliable source that knows. Gamble has recordings of Jihad talking to Dave Battle about shit that he shouldn't be speaking on. He's telling Save a rack of shit that you been doing and he's mentioning my fuckin' name, too. They know that he has a cellphone and all that shit. He told Dave about you killing the bitch at Maylord—"

"The bitch that was with Baby E?"

"That too, but I'm talking specifically about the other one… Tosheka Jennings. Your ex-girlfriend… And P.G. is building a case on you about that. Then there's the Woodmore Town Center joints. He mentioned both of us. My man says that the actual recording can't hurt us because Gamble planted the bus in Jihad… he says that Dave's cell is probably bugged too... illegally and can't use them in court. But he says that the recordings are pointing all the wrong people in the right directions. His words exactly. And to make matters worse, they got another rat named Joshua Clark telling them that Doo Doo told him that I killed Crud and you killed Whistle. Either way this shit goes, youngin, there's only one outcome for me and that's death. I'm not going back to prison, I'm not letting myself be arrested. It's carried by six than judged by twelve for me. So, real talk, I don't give a fuck. Your brother running his mouth so loosely can only affect you. I still got love somewhere in my body for you and that's why I'm giving you the heads up about Jihad. And this is the last time I'ma do this. Everything after this is on you." I turned to exit the car, but stopped in my tracks. "I found out who killed my daughter, too."

"Who was it?" Quran asked.

I turned and faced Quran and laughed.

CHAPTER 3

QURAN

"I found out who killed my daughter, too."

"Who was it?" I asked.

Sean turned to face me and laughed. His mask of grief was disguised by a smile that made him appear Joker like. "Renaissance Tyler. Turns out that the red haired bitch is the female version of me. She's a vicious killer just like her father. I underestimated her. I got cocky and it cost my baby her life. While I was lacking and looking for Ren Tyler, she was looking for me. She couldn't find me so she found Shontay. I'm on her ass, though, youngin. What she don't know is that she fucking with the best. Everybody last name Tyler is about to die, then Rodney and his family, then the remaining Clarks. After them is the most important kill."

"And who is that, old head?"

"Michael Maurice Carter."

"You might never get to kill Mike Carter, slim. If he gets released, I might beat you to it."

"Been thinking about everything I told you, huh?"

"Yeah, but I just found out that your suspicions were right. Zin has a letter her mother wrote before she died. In that letter she predicted her own death. She believed that Mike would order her death and use me and Dontay to do it. She admitted that she loved my father and that they were fucking. She believed that Mike caught them in bed one night and for that he killed my father. You said it, Patricia Carter said it. That makes two people saying the same shit and that's enough for me. Mike Carter is a dead man walking."

Sean smiled. "Doesn't matter to me who kills the serpent as long as he dies. I'll contact you if I need to but I doubt that I will." The smile left Sean's face, then he turned and got out of the car.

I sat and watched Sean from my rear-view mirror. He walked to the Toyota pickup and disappeared inside. Seconds later, the Toyota pulled out of its spot and vanished. My thoughts went to everything Sean had just said about Jihad and his cell being bugged.

"Muthafucka!" I hissed and smacked the steering wheel. Greg Gamble had gone too far this time. My blood boiled inside my veins. "That's it! Ain't no more passes. I'm kill your ass, Gamble! Watch!"

Central Treatment Facility
1901 E. Street S.E.

Tomasina walked out the jail and spotted me standing beside the car. The cold was biting, but I ignored it. Wind struck up suddenly and blew Tomasina's hair around giving her the look of an apparition in a scary movie. She beelined for me.

"Quran... what the fuck, boy! What was so important that I had to drop everything and come—"

"Jihad and Dave's cells are bugged." I said suddenly.

"What?" Tomasina asked, face registering different emotions at once. "What did you just say?"

"You heard me. Jihad and Dave's cells are bugged. Completely wired for sound."

Tomasina shook her head. "Ain't no way. You paranoid Qur—"

I stepped up close to Tomasina. So close that I could smell the fruit smell on her breath. "Listen to me, Tom. If I tell you

26

that a duck can pull a truck, don't ever question me, just hook the duck to the truck. If I tell you that the sky is green look at it until you can see the green. And don't ever call me paranoid again. Do you understand me?"

Tomasina nodded.

"The U.S. Attorney for D.C. is a wicked muthafucka. He has a personal axe to grind with my associates, me, my brother, our father… Allah bless the dead… and my friends. He wants me more than anything. He's a dirty pool playing nigga. He don't play by no rules at no times. I got friends in place you wouldn't believe, Tom. And one of those friends just told me that Dave and Jihad's cells are bugged. He heard the recordings and told me what was said, so I know it's true. I need you to go back in there and get both of them niggas phones and flush 'em. Break 'em up and flush them. Then—" I reached in my pocket and pulled out two letters. I handed both letters to Tomasina. "I need you to give both Dave and Jay their letters. Tell them that this ain't a drill, shit is real. Can you do that for me?" Before Tomasina could answer, I pulled out a wad of cash and passed it to her. "Make it happen!" Without a word, I turned, got into the car and left.

CHAPTER 4

TOMASINA

"Samuels... Where are you coming from?" Captain Jake Stevens asked as he stood by the metal detector near the employee entrance to CTF. "It damn sure ain't your lunch break time."

Thinking fast, she said the first thing that came to her mind. "If you must know, Captain Stevens, I came on my period a day earlier. There was blood and shit in my clothes—"

"Okay, okay, Samuels, enough said. Too much information. Just get back to your post, would you?"

Smiling inside, I replied, "Yes sir. Right away, sir. Just had to change pants and get some tampons—"

"I said that's enough info, Samuels. Damn!" Captain Stevens walked off.

"Thomas, what you laughing at?"

Theodore Thomas continued to laugh despite hearing the question. "I'm laughing at your ass, Samuels. You know good and got damn well that was a lie you just told Stevens. I'm hip to your lil Sexy ass."

"True that, baby boy. Saying shit like you just said might get you some of me one day." I said as I walked through the checkpoint.

"Get me some? Get me some what? Just because I called you sexy don't mean I want none. Unless you got a dick down there, too. You a hermaphrodite, Samuels?

"Damn, Thomas, who knew? Sorry, baby, ain't no dick in my pants. There might be one in me later on, though."

"You too?" Officer Thomas replied and laughed.

"Bye, Thomas. With your crazy ass. Later."

"Later Samuels. And it ain't too late for you to become a Cowboys fan. D.C stands for Dallas Cowboys… but in my case, it stands for Dick Chaser!"

* * *

After copying the letters, I folded the originals back the way that Quran had given them to me. I even added a piece of tape on both. I pocketed the two copies after folding them and putting the other two in a different pocket. Looking at my watch, I left Unit DB4 and went to the medical unit. Inside the office I gave Toshanda Whitaker, the office on duty two one hundred dollar bills.

"What's this for, Tom?" Toshanda asked.

"I need to talk to one of the inmates. Not in his cell, though. I need like 15 minutes with him in the exam room. All you have to do is pop him out and send him to the room. The shift lieutenant already made his rounds. We should be good. If anything goes wrong, I'll take the whole beef. Tell 'em I popped him out and all that shit."

Toshanda looked shook. "I don't know, Tom. I ain't never did no shit like this before. What if—"

"You wasting time, Shonda. All I need is 15 minutes with him. And I'ma add three hundred to that two. That's five hundred dollars to just let me see my friend for 15 minutes."

"Okay, Tom. Who is the inmate?"

"Jihad Bashir."

* * *

"CO Samuels, what's good with you?" Jihad asked as soon as the examination room door closed.

I looked at Quran's brother and couldn't get over how much he looked just like Quran. Looking at his light grey eyes made my pussy wet. "I got a message for you from your brother, but first I want some of that dick. Are you as big as Quran, Jihad?" Jihad Bashir smiled and pulled out his dick from his pants. "Bigger."

"Sit down in that chair right there. I'll be the judge of that." I unfastened my belt and pulled my pants and panties to my ankles. "We ain't got much time. So, don't take long to bust."

"You got a rubber for me?" Jihad asked.

"Don't need one. I'm disease-free. What about you?" I replied, turned and sat down on Jihad's hard on. I bounced up and down a few times before Jihad gripped my waist and held me down on his dick to grind himself deeper in me. "O-o-o-h shit! Damn nigga! You might be bigger!"

* * *

Quickly, I got myself fixed up after letting Jihad bust his nut inside of me. "Cum gon' be running out of me all night." I said, then turned to face Jihad again, his pants now up. "Quran says to tell you and David that y'all cells are bugged,"

"What? Bugged? How in the —"

"Look, don't kill the messenger. He said that he has an inside connection and that source has heard you talking to David in the cell about shit you're not supposed to be talking about. He's adamant about both of y'all cells being wired for sound! He wants you to get rid of the cell phones and to stop talking in or out of your cells. That's the message he told me to give y'all verbally." I reached into my pocket and pulled

IF YOU CROSS ME ONCE 6 | ANTHONY FIELDS

out the letters Quran gave me. "These letters are for y'all. You and David—"

"But how… who would bug our cells?"

"Damn, I'm glad you asked that because I almost forgot. Quran said that the U.S. Attorney dud Greg Gamble had y'all cells bugged. Illegally, but he did it nonetheless. That's all Quran said. I gave you the letters. Get David his because I'm not gonna be able to pull him out to give it to him myself. I gotta go before someone catches me and you in here. Get rid of the cellphone. Tell David to do the same. Quran's orders. And no more talking about street shit, past or present, in or out of the cells." He said that this is not a drill."

"I got you. Tell bruh, I'm sorry—"

"Tell him yourself when all of this blows over. Fix your clothes and come on."

* **

At my post, I pulled out the letters Quran sent to David and Jihad. I read them both one more time. The letters could be used as collateral for a blackmail if need be. But then my common sense kicked in. There was no blackmailing a man like Quran Bashir. A man whose heart turned to stone at times. My plan was to kill Quran not the other way around. I took the copies of the letters and balled them up. Then I pretended to be shooting jumpers on the basketball court as I discarded them into the waste basket. After a few minutes of thought, I fished the letters out of the trash can and put them back in my pocket. There were other ways that Quran's own words on paper might come in handy.

IF YOU CROSS ME ONCE 6 | ANTHONY FIELDS

CHAPTER 5

ZIN

Zin's Condo

"Quran, slow down! Calm down! Tell me again what's got you so bothered! What did Greg Gamble do this time?"

Quran paced the living room floor talking to himself. His coat and hat lay in a heap near the door. He pulled off his sweatshirt and tossed it on the couch. The shoestrings on his Timberland boots were untied. "I should've been did it. I should've been smoked his ass. Shouldn't have waited so long. Shouldn't have ever listened to Sean. It's my fault. Should've went with my first instinct and yours. I got him, though. I'ma fuck his foggie ass around real proper. How can I find out where Gamble live at?" Quran suddenly stopped pacing, turned to me and asked.

I shrugged my shoulders. "I don't know. I guess his home address wouldn't be public information. I guess we could look online—"

"Don't even worry about it. I'ma find him. I might have to follow him home when he gets off work. It'll be better to kill him away from downtown."

"You're scaring me, Quran. What happened?"

I talked to Sean today. Met him at the Harris Teeters at Crystal City. He told me that Greg Gamble has my brother's cell at CTF bugged. His and Dave's—"

"Bugged? He can't do that. Unless he got a warrant to put a listening device in their cells and he hasn't. David's my client, I would know… wait... maybe not, but why would he bug their cells in the first place?"

"To get information and according to Sean, stupid ass Jihad is doing just that."

"But… Baby, how in the hell would Sean know something like that? About cells being bugged at CTF?"

"He said he has a source. I believe him. Dave got stabbed over at the jail and I knew exactly who stabbed him 48 hours later. I have someone inside CTF that can get anything I want to Jay and Dave in 24 hours. I know shit that I'm not supposed to know because I know people in all the right places. Apparently, so does Sean. He's been grief stricken and lunchin' like shit about his mother and daughter. All the murders that have been on the news lately… that's him. That's Sean out there bodying shit to satisfy his appetite for destruction. Then all of a sudden, after days with no contact, he contacts me to tell me that Jay is in his cell at CTF talking too fuckin much and to who. Sean says he doesn't care about Jihad talking because he's gonna make the cops kill him if they get too close to him. Says he's not letting no cops arrest him. He's not going back to jail, he says. He said he surfaced to give ME a warning. This warning being that Jihad's cell is bugged and that Jihad is talking about shit that's gonna land me in jail for life. He mentioned Tosheka and the fact that P.G. County cops are building a case against me for her murder—"

"But we already know that."

"Yeah, we did. Sean didn't. He also said that they're building a case against me about four people killed at Woodmere Town Center."

"You knew that, too."

"Again, I did. But Sean didn't. I don't think. Ever since his daughter got killed… ever since Shontay died… Anyway,

Sean said that the bug was put there illegally and it's useless in court."

"He's right about that. But why would Gamble get someone to bug Jihad's cell and possibly David's cell for information that he can't use? No matter what he learns from the audio on the bugs, he can't use it. So, why even go through all the trouble—"

"Sean says that although the recordings from the bugs can't be used in court, they are pointing all the wrong people in the right directions."

"Well, if that's what they're for, then I can see the purpose of them. Question, though. You've known for almost a year now that Greg Gamble wants your head…well, not only your head, but our heads. Jihad's and my father's as well, on a plate, why are you so bent out of shape to learn that he's done some more underhanded shit to reach his goal? I mean… look at all the shit he's already done. To my father, to Sean Branch, to Khitab, to David, to me and to you. Why the hundred pounds of anger and disbelief now all of a sudden. Why the urge to kill him now? After all he's already done?"

"Because enough is enough. I guess something inside me thought that he might ease up. That he might find something else to do besides worry so much about us. I guess I thought that as time went on, he'd lose his desire to see me behind bars. Today, I learned that I was wrong on every front. Today, I realized that if I don't do something about Greg Gamble, Greg Gamble is going to do something about ME. As plain as the nose on my face. If your father is gonna ever really be free and if Dave is gonna come home and live his life. If Jihad is ever gonna get out of jail and have a life, if you and I are gonna be allowed to live in peace and raise our child in this world, Gregory Gamble cannot be alive in it!"

* * *

Later that night…

34

"... at night, when you're far and I'm alone/ I feel the fabric from your T-shirt blowing through my thighs. I can still hear your baritone telling me you'll take it slow/ and I was in the mirror playing roles, like you were here, I couldn't turn me on/ So, I, fell asleep with the music on/ woke up again hearing the same old song playing, saying / give it to me deeper/ you giving me the fever/ now you got my feet up/ this one is a keeper/ now the second verse is playing—"

The Destiny's Child song playing in the room seemed to be written just for me as Quran did anything possible to make me orgasm, over and over again. The music drowned out my moans of ecstasy and fulfillment.

"... give it to me deeper/ now you got my feet up/ hold me while my hands up/ when the music cuts off/ fantasies will shut off/ I'm thinking to myself again/ when you're not here, I sleep in your T-shirt/ after we make love, I'll sleep in your T-shirt/ wake up in your T-shirt/ to smell the scent of your cologne—"

If making love to your woman was an Olympic event, Quran would take the gold medal every time. I half listened to Beyonce, Kelly and Michelle sing as my body floated to the ceiling and stayed there. All I could do was look down at myself on the bed. My right leg up and held in place by Quran's powerful left arm. I could see my toes curling and straightening up as he pounded into me. I could see my left leg, open and bent at the knee. I could see the sweat an Quran's back, the muscles bulging, his toned butt cheeks rise and fall slowly, powerfully. I could see the look on my face. I could recognize my furrow of my brow and the opening of my mouth. I could hear the sounds that left my mouth. I could feel what my body felt. It was like heaven on earth.

* * *

"What's on your plate for today?" I asked Quran as I stood at the stove making us breakfast.

35

"A little bit of the same shit from yesterday. Street shit. You?"

"Appointments, meetings, research. And I plan on visiting my father today."

"That's what's up." Wuran replied while looking at his plate. "And speaking of yesterday, I hope that you were just emotional and venting last night. A lot has changed since we talked about Greg Gamble dying. You have too much to lose to really try and kill that man. Hopefully, a good night's sleep and some good pussy—"

"Great pussy. Get it right."

"I'm not giving you any this morning, so no need to run game on me, sir. I hope that great pussy and some rest has settled you down and made you more reasonable—"

"Reasonable" Quran said, stood up and walked over to me. He reached around me and grabbed a strip of turkey bacon out of the pan. He chewed it as if it wasn't piping hot. "The rest was needed and so was that great sex and bomb head—"

I elbowed Quran without looking behind me.

"O-ooww," he said and laughed. "I hear what you're saying, baby girl and I feel you, but my mind is made up. Greg Gamble is a dead man walking. Him and the rest of the world just doesn't know it yet."

CHAPTER 6

JIHAD

Central Treatment Facility
Medical Unit
8:43 a.m.

"Are you sure?" Dave asked me.

Standing near the shower area that was deserted, I looked at my street homie like he was retarded. "What the fuck kinda question is that? Am I sure? How am I not gonna be sure. The word came directly from Tomasina after she talked to Bruh. You read the letter he sent you, right? So, yeah of course I'm sure. Ain't you?"

"Did you fuck her?"

"What?"

"You heard me. Did you fuck her?"

"Who? Tomasina?"

Dave nodded.

"Why does that even matter, Slim?"

"Yeah, you fucked her."

I laughed, despite my anger building. "Aye, Slim... you can't be serious right now. I just told you that both of our cells have been bugged by Greg Gamble and that he got a recording or recordings of us talking about bodies and shit and all you concerned about is whether or not I fucked the C. O. bitch? You gotta be fuckin' playing with me right now. Slim. Tell me that you playing."

37

"Fuck all that. Tell me again everything that the bitch told you." Dave demanded. I relayed the message that Tomasina gave me for a second time to Dave. "That's what she said word for word."

"I wonder why she pulled you out instead of me?"

"Get rid of the jack, Slim. ASAP." I said and turned my back on Dave. He was pissing me off and I needed to leave before things got ugly between us. I walked back into my cell and looked all over for a device that I could see. It was the third time I had looked. After finding nothing. I strained my vision to see if I could see into the vent above my sink. I couldn't. Hopping down off the sink, I said to myself, "Gotta be in the vent. That's why maintenance was in the chase closet days ago like that." I laid on the bunk and tried to remember everything I had said to Dave inside my cell. Shaking my head, I thought about all the things I'd told him while we smoked. I'd basically told Dave everything that he couldn't have known about the streets and what happened since he'd been in jail.

"Damn!" I muttered to myself as I thought about all the shit I had said over the days I'd been at CTF. All the wild shit I'd said on phone calls to niggas and a few women. I thought instantly about what the Holy Quran said about protecting the private pests and the tongue. Suddenly another thought hit me. It was something that Dave had said to me a couple of days ago...

"One of these niggas in here talking, Slim." Dave said.

"Why you say that?" I asked.

"Because them muthafuckas... the cops been in my cell twice in the last 3 days. Then the maintenance people was in my chase closet in between my cell twice this morning. Bitches probably bugged my cell."

"Or you can just be being paranoid, Big Homie."

"Maybe. Maybe not—"

I got out the bunk and went to find Dave. I found him in his cell. He looked up as he saw me enter the cell, then went back to what he was doing. Flushing broken pieces of the cellphone down the toilet. Silently, I waited until he was done and motioned for him to leave the cell with me. Outside in the day room, I said, "Remember what you said to me the other day?"

Dave shrugged and threw up his hands. "I said a lot of shit to you the other day."

"I'm talking about when you told me that someone was snitching because the cops had been in your cell twice in three days? And how the maintenance niggas been in your chase closet twice—"

"Yeah, yeah... I remember that." Suddenly, the light came on inside of Dave's head. "Damn... I was right. I told you that they probably bugged my cell and I was right. You said that I was just being paranoid. I was fuckin right the whole time. Bitch ass niggas! Greg Gamble strikes again. That nigga won't let up, first he files a motion with the court to let my dead witnesses testimonies still be used at trial. Then he tries to get me to be a rat when he showed up at the infirmary after I busted that creep nigga. He got his people to try and cook me on that gun charge in front of Judge Bergel. He tryna charge me with attempted murder, naw that gun charge is done. And still he's not satisfied. His foggie ass done bugged my cell tryna see what I say that he can use against me—"

"Our cell. He bugged our cells and speaking of which... I just remembered something."

"What?"

"Me and you talked about your case in my cell. That day when you asked me what was going on out there and I told you. Remember that? You walked in my cell and said, "I wanna leave everything that y'all couldn't tell me over the phone. Starting with Tabu, ending with Tosheka."

"Damn!," Dave exclaimed and covered his face.

For a long time, neither Dave nor I said a word.

"I asked you all that stupid ass shit about all the witnesses in my case and you answered all my fuckin' questions. They might reopen my case on the body—"

"And try to charge me and Bruh with all the murders. We fucked up."

"But, wait… didn't you say that the bitch said that Que said that the bug was planted illegally and that they can't use any of what we said against us?"

"Yeah, that's what she said, but how do we know for sure?" I asked.

Dave shook his head in exasperation. "Loose lips sink ships. We know better. Que is probably pissed off like shit at us."

"Agreed. And when Bruh gets pissed, people die. You gotta talk to him. Check his temperature."

"I gotta talk to him? I gotta check his temperature? Why me?" Dave asked.

"Well, one of us needs to talk to Bruh and fast before we both end up on a cold slab in the morgue. If he feels that we've said too much and it threatens his freedom, you already know what comes next. He proved that with Tabu."

"How do we reach him? Through the bitch?"

I moved some furniture around in my head. Then the answer hit me. "Zin. We need to get in touch with Zin."

"Did you get rid of that letter that Que sent you?" Dave asked suddenly.

"Of course, I did. Right after I read it, I flushed it. You did the same, right?"

Dave nodded.

"Did your letter say the same things as mine?"

"Yeah, to flush the phone and to stop running my fuckin' mouth so much."

"He gon' kill us, Slim."

"I already know."

CHAPTER 7

GREG GAMBLE

United States Attorney's Office
555 4th St. N.W.

"The U. S. House of Representatives passed a bill that would permanently restrict the D.C. City Council from enacting any legislation charging sentencing laws, even to make them harsher. A move that local leaders say could drastically curtail their ability to respond to crime trends in the city."

"This bill would be the biggest rollback of D.C. self-governance in a generation," Delegate Elener Jones Foreman said in a speech on the House floor.

Eighteen Democrats joined Republicans to pass the legislation by a vote of 225 to 181, showing how bi-partisan concerns following last year's crime spike, which in some ways directly impacted lawmakers, continue to linger. The legislation called the D.C. Crimes Act– or the D.C. Criminal Reforms to Immediately Make Everyone Safer Act, is part of the House Republicans aggressive oversight of D.C. At at time when juvenile crime has been in the spotlight in D.C., the bill would also seek to harden punishment for youth offenders, by removing some options for leniency from judge's discretion. Reflective of House Republicans frequent refrain that D.C. is soft on crime.

"This bill requires that we treat adult criminals as adults, like the rest of the country does." The bill's sponsor Bill Donovan, a Republican for Florida, had to say. "The legislation would face more hurdles in the Democratic controlled Senate, requiring 60 votes to advance. The White House has said that the President strongly opposes the bill. Still, a trio of elected District leaders expressed significant concerns in a letter to House leadership Wednesday. Citing the permanent impact that restricting the District from making changes to sentencing laws could home role and local crime response. Under the bill, on Congress, which has oversight over D.C. under the Constitution, would be allowed to change D.C. sentencing laws which D.C. leaders argue would be an unreliable and ineffective system—"

Someone knocked once on my office door and then entered the room. It was Ian McNeely.

"Hate to interrupt you—"

"Sit down, Ian. You need to see the rest of this," I demanded.

"What is it?" Ian replied, before taking a seat near me.

"The news."

"This bill would prevent District policy makers from responding to emerging crime trends, by enhancing criminal penalties or even create new crimes. "Mayor Mary Bowman, D.C. Councilman Allen Charles and Attorney General Brad Shaub wrote in a letter to House leadership.

"Swift and certain consequences are essential to deterring crime. Persistent congressional interference is at odds with that goal."

"The legislation would amend D.C.'s Home Rule charter to prohibit future changes to sentencing laws, though Republicans say that it will not prevent creating new crimes. It also targets the 1985 Youth Rehabilitation Act, which allows judges to grant higher sentences to certain young adults under 25 and set their convictions aside if they complete their sentence. Donovan's bill would cut off

IF YOU CROSS ME ONCE 6 | ANTHONY FIELDS

eligibility for the more lenient treatment at 18 years old. Donovan previously said he was introducing the bill because the D.C. City Council wasn't doing its job. Saying at a hearing in March that if the D.C. Council is not going to act, Congress does have a responsibility to act in the interest of the District of Columbia. But the timing of Donovan's bill was curious to the Democratic D.C. officials. The House Oversight Committee held a hearing on the bill two days after the D.C. Council passed the SECURE D.C. Act, an omnibus crime bill that amongst other things, enhanced penalties for gun offenses and expanded pretrial detention for those charged with violent crimes—"

"I'm already familiar with this, boss—" Ian McNeely said.

"Are you?" I replied. "So, tell me, Ian, is Bill Donovan's bill a good thing or a bad thing for D.C.?"

"Uh... a good thing. I've been following this for a minute because of the implications the bill will have on our office. The D.C. Council is out of touch with crime and crime trends. This bill... CRIMES ACT—"

"D.C. CRIMES ACT—"

"Excuse me, D.C. CRIMES ACT is a filibuster that is greatly needed to make sure that citizens of D.C. can be safe—"

"Why do I get the feeling that you are referencing D.C. burgeoning white citizenry law in your spiel? I don't get the feeling that any of the native citizens of D.C. matter to you or the Bill Donovans of the world."

Ian McNeely's face turned beet red. He stood up. "I resent that implication, Greg! It's racist... and...and—"

"True, Ian. Sanctimonious theatrics aside, you don't see the D.C. I see, Ian. You can't. You see the new D.C., the gentrified mostly white D.C. I see the old D.C., the Chocolate City D.C. You're from where, Ian? What state in the U. S.?"

"Delaware. I'm from Dover, Delaware. Why?"

"But you live here now, right? In D.C. or its surrounding area?"

"Right here in the city. Near the Navy Yard."

"Great. And how much do you really know about D.C., Ian?"

"I...I...I think I know a fair amount about this city."

"Probably. But do you know that the whole of D.C. only encompasses sixty-nine square miles in diameter?"

"Sixty-nine square miles? Uh... no... And that's important, why?"

"Because I was born and raised here, Ian. And every one of those sixty nine square miles is embedded in me. And although, I'm often at odds with the D.C. City Council when it comes to policing, crime and policy in D.C., I do believe in the Council's right to exist. And D.C.'s right to self-governance. There is no way in God's green Special Earth that Bill fucking Donovan from Jacksonville, Florida should be sponsoring a bill that effects policy, good or bad, in these sixty-nine square miles that I live in. I am more than appalled at the way Congress... well, the House wants to usurp the D.C. Council's control of how and when this city changes it's laws. What did you want to tell me, Ian?"

"Uh... why did I come in here? Oh... I just received word from a reliable source that Judge Hamilton has already made up his mind to overturn Michael Carter's conviction and to release him on high intensity supervision until we decide whether or not we want to retry him."

"We are not going to retry Michael. That ship has sailed."

"I already know that. You've told me that several times. So, what is our position on it? At least for news sound bite purposes? Are we just quietly capitulating here or loudly acquiescing? What's your next move?"

"There is no next move, Ian. It's over. We lost. Michael Carter goes free and the scandal surrounding Michael Carter continues. We make no statement to the media. No comments because of the ongoing investigations. Very real investigations. I received word today from a reliable source, too. I am going to be summoned to meet with three people in the next week or so. Attorney General Brad Shoub, Stephen Ross from Justice and Matt Ryan who heads the Office of Professional Responsibility. So, forgive me, if I'm not taken aback by the news that Judge 'Cut Em Loose' Bruce Hamilton is going to release Michael Carter. Thank you for stopping by." I turned my attention back to the T.V. monitor…

"Had the D.C. CRIMES Act of 2014 been enacted earlier, it would have blocked the District's increases to criminal penalties. The D.C. CRIMES Act is a counterproductive and invasion of the District's right to self-governance. And it would impede public safety and crime reduction. This bill highlights why the District of Columbia should have Statehood—"

Grabbing the remote off of my desk, I clicked the T.V. off. Inside my desk drawer was my cellphone. I retrieved it. I dialed a number. Donovan Olsen answered quickly. "Don, it's me."

"What can I do for you, Greg?"

"Find out everything new you can about our Attorney General—"

"Paul Danielson?"

"Yes. And I need what you can gather on short notice about Stephen Ross at the Department of Justice. There's only one there, I checked. Dig up whatever you can find on him."

"Is that all you need?" Donovan asked.

"That's all for now. I have a file on Matt Ryan over at OPR already. Get back to me with everything you can find as quickly as you can."

* * *

I listened to the recordings on the thumb drive. None of what David Battle said in his cell or on his cellphone was of any use to me.

"All this muthafucka does is have phone sex all fucking day!" I muttered upset.

Having David Battles' cell bugged had proven a waste of time and resources. I thought about Bruce Culbreath and how bitchy his attitude had been when he'd brought me the thumb drive. His petulant ravings and rantings made me wonder who was the gay man, me or him."

"I listened to the recordings, Greg. There's nothing on them." Bruce whined. "Well, at least nothing for you to use. On the other hand, I've learned lots. The device recorded also the intercom system in the cell. Battle or Bashir have been called out and had their cell doors popped numerous times in the last few weeks. That means that officers on my staff have been pulling them both out and giving them contraband. They've had a couple different cell phones given to them and God knows how much drugs and what not. I'm authorizing a full scale... a mass shake down of the medical unit and I am going to question the officers on duty each—"

"You'll do no such thing, Bruce." I said calmly.

"What? Don't you fucking tell me how to do—"

"Bruce, I will not let you fuck up what I am building against those two men. Who gives a flying fuck about cellphones and dugs. Both jails... CTF and CDF are filled with that shit. Your staff has been bringing contraband into both facilities since the eighties. Ten years ago, I tried to fight that shit. We sent MECCA LEE-BEY into the D.C. jail with one purpose. To gather info on what CO's were bringing in drugs and cellphones. And what did we learn, Bruce? Huh? We learned that ALL the fucking CO's were guilty. Right up to the captains and majors. So much so that we couldn't hold them all responsible. Had we done that, we would have had to close the whole gotdamn facility because there would have been no staff left to operate it. So, don't

stand here and get overly sanctimonious on me! Jihad Bashir and David Battle are not making weapons. They are not recruiting people to join ISIS. They are not killing other inmates. They are talking on cellphones and smoking weed. Get the fuck over it, will you! The bugs stay. No lockdown, no shakedowns, no staff round ups. Or you my friend will be the next topic on the local news. Not just me. Am I clear?"

Smiling, I thought about Bruce Culbreath's face as he capitulated to me. Information is power and I had plenty of it. I listened again to the recordings from both men's cells. Other than the first recordings from Jihad Bashir's cell, there'd been no tantalizing tidbits. A knock on my door caught my attention. Silently, I prayed that Ian McNeely wasn't at the door again. "Come in."

My prayers weren't answered. Ian McNeely walked through my door with a young woman in tow. "Greg, I have someone here that I want you to meet." Ian turned to the woman. "Introduce yourself to my boss."

"My… name… I'm… I'm Daychelle Spencer."

I stood up from my desk and walked around it. "Hi, Daychelle, I'm Greg Gamble." I looked at Ian.

"Greg, you remember my CI Kendra Dyson, right?" Ian asked.

"I nodded. "KD from Sursum Cordas. Killed recently near Union Station—"

"I was there" the woman named Daychelle blurted out.

"Hear her out first, Greg and then I'll tell you why she's here in your office."

I nodded again. "Okay. Would you like to sit down, Daychelle? Can I get you anything?"

"I want to stand up. And naw, I'm good."

"Day Day, tell my boss everything that you told me earlier," Ian told the woman.

The woman was beautiful, cinnamon complexioned with freckles and gorgeous hazel brown eyes. Her hair was dyed two shades of brown and light brown and styled perfectly.

"About a week ago, me, KD and my friend Marshay were at a party. Not really a party, more like a get-together. Our girl Deja always had lil get-togethers. While we were there, this guy named Scam-bino—"

"Scam…who?" I asked.

"Scam-bino. That's his nickname, though. His real name is Andy. Andy Daniels. Scam-bino… introduced us to a dude he said was his cousin. The dude was fine as shit. He wanted to buy some weed from KD. Asked for a sample, so we smoked with him. He liked the weed. He told Kendra that he wanted twenty pounds of it. Tried to get he to come down on the price. But she wouldn't. She never did. For anybody. He said that he was from Kenworth but hung out in Glassmanor. Named a lot of street dudes who could vouch for him. KD…Kendra put his number in her phone and they agreed to hook up later. Two things happened after that. Both of them strange to me. When we were inside of Deja's apartment talking to the dude—"

"The dude from Kenworth, who wanted to buy the twenty pounds of weed from KD?" I asked and wrote down everything I was being told.

Daychelle nodded. "Right. Him. Anyway, the whole time he was talking to us, he seemed distracted. He was whispering to Andy and looking at JoJo—"

"JoJo?"

"Yeah. JoJo Morris. Joseph Morris. He was some kin to Mae Cheeks and Moose. The dude kept looking at JoJo. After him and KD exchanged numbers, he left. Not long after him, Scam-bino... Andy and JoJo left the apartment. Minutes later, we heard gunshots outside. Later that day, we found out that JoJo got killed at the back of the Tyler House building. Me, KD and Shay… that's my friend Marshay… talked about the coincidence of what happened, but dismissed it. We all know that JoJo had a lot of enemies and rumored to have money on his head for snitching on some dudes. A couple days later, the dude calls KD and wants to meet to get the weed. She told him to meet her at the Union Station bus depot, where the Greyhound buses pick up and drop people off. Kendra and I ride in my Caddy… I had a CTV-S coupe… All black. Kendra was in the passenger seat, I drove. Shay was behind us in KD's Jaguar SUV. The twenty pounds of weed was in the Jaguar with Shay. When we pulled up, we didn't know what car he'd be in. We just pulled in and KD called his phone. The next thing I know, a dud appears dressed in all black and opens fire on the car. I screamed and ducked… but…but KD got caught off guard. The window exploded and she got hit. It happened so fast. Shay pulled off and I saw the Jaguar leave us. I sat there until the policy came. Kendra wasn't breathing. There was blood and brain—"

"Okay, Day Day." Ian said, cutting the woman off. "What was the guy's name that y'all went there to meet?"

"He was Andy's cousin. He said his name was… well, Andy said his name was Quintez or Quintay or something like that. But his nickname was Que."

At the mention of the nickname Que, I stopped writing and gave the woman my undivided attention. "And what does Que look like, Daychelle?"

"We called him Pretty Boy at the apartment because he was so fine. He was tall, about 6 feet tall with an almond complexion. He had dark black curly hair and the prettiest grey eyes I … we had ever seen. He looked muscular… medium build, uh… that's all I remember.

I glanced over at Ian McNeely who smiled a mischievous grin. The woman had just described Quran Bashir. "If I show you a picture of a guy who fits that description… Better yet, Ian, prepare me a line up… one page, six photos. You know who I'm thinking about, correct? Who Que might be?"

"I do. That's why Daychelle is standing in your office. I'll be right back" Ian replied and left.

"Daychelle, Ian is going to return with a photo array. I want you to look at it and see if you recognize anyone on it, okay?"

"Okay." Daychelle replied.

"And just for the record, you didn't see who the person was who shot and killed KD, correct?"

"Correct. I just know that we went there to meet Scambino's cousin, Que."

"And this same man, Scam-bino… Andy Daniels' cousin Que was at the Tyler House building on the night that Joseph 'Jo Jo' Morris was killed, correct?"

"Um-hm. But I didn't see him kill nobody."

"Right. And just out of curiosity, how did you come to tell Ian McNeely your story? I mean how do you know Ian?"

"I'm his confidential informant. I watched Kendra for him. Informed on all the people that she did business with."

"How long have you been an informant for Ian?"

"For about 3 and a half years."

On cue, Ian walked back into the office. He handed a single sheet of paper to Daychelle.

"Do you recognize anybody… any picture in that photo array?"

Daychelle looked at the photo array and quickly said, "Yeah. This is him. That's Que."

Ian and I both hurried to Daychelle's side to see who she'd chosen. A broad smile erupted on my face. "Are you sure that's him, Daychelle?" I asked.

Daychelle nodded. "I'm positive. I could never forget him."

The man that Daychelle picked out was none other than Quran Bashir.

CHAPTER 8

MICHAEL CARTER

Central Detention Facility
(D.C. Jail)
"How are you adjusting to the DMV?"

Valencia Burrow's exhaled. "It's been a little rough with trying to get acclimated to the streets, this traffic and just trying to find little shit. But overall, I'm good. Glad to finally get away from St. Louis. Been there my entire life and I was in desperate need of a change. So, thank you so much for that."

"Don't mention it baby. The way you been holding me down for the last five years or more, I owe you—"

"You don't owe me anything, Mike. I keep telling you that."

"And I keep telling you that I do. You don't understand what you mean to me. After I was convicted for a murder that I didn't commit, my mental state was a little shaky. I went through the whole spectrum of emotions. All I had to keep me sane was the love I got from my daughter and my sister. All the women that I took care of and broke bread with, figured I was washed up. They left and said, 'fuck Mike;. Not literally, but it sure felt that way. I've met different women over the years, pretty much the same way I met you. All the good men wanted to hook me up with women they knew. But nothing clicked with them. Then Mujahid introduced me to you."

"Jerome Williams is the brother I never had. He knows me better than anyone despite the fact that he been in prison since he was a juvenile. When he first called and told me about his old head from D.C, I was skeptical. I was apprehensive. I wasn't really looking to start anything new with anyone. Let alone a dud in jail, you feel me?"

"I definitely feel you."

"But I decided to let go and let God decide what happened. And you turned out to be just what the life doctor ordered. I gotta write Jerome again and thank him—"

"No need for that. Muja knows he did a good thing. I remind him of it all the time. He called my phone yesterday. Where are you now?"

"I'm in the house. Just got back here. Saw this adult store I wanted to visit. So, I went," Val said.

"Adult store?" I asked.

"Yeah. It's one of them stores for adults only. They type of place that sell sex toys and erotic shit for couples. I found some things that I'ma try on you when I get home."

"Is that right? What did you get?"

"The prerequisite— sexy lingerie, garters, stockings and crotchless panties. In all different colors. I got mood candles, massage cream and oils, massagers, vibrators, other toys and handcuffs."

"Handcuffs? Uh... I don't know about that."

Val laughed. "I know, I know. You've been in enough handcuffs to last for a lifetime. They're not for you. I want you to cuff me."

The thought of me handcuffing anybody made me laugh.

"I'm serious, Mike. So stop laughing. I want... I want—"

"What do you want, Val?"

"I want you to handcuff each of my wrists to a bed post so that I can't get away. And I want you to eat this pussy until my juices and com coat your mustache, lips and cheeks. I want you to lick my inner thighs until I beg you to suck on my clit. After I've cum again for the third or fourth time, then I want you to climb in between my legs and put your dick in me deep. I want you to fuck me rough. I want you to put both of my feet on your shoulders and fuck me until I can't take the dick anymore. That's what I want.

"That's what you want, huh? What are you wearing right now?"

"Just the sweater I wore today and panties."

"Take that sweater off."

"Okay."

"It's off."

"Mm-hmm."

"You got them big pretty titties out?"

"Mmm-hmmmm—"

"That pussy wet?"

"Mmm…hmmmm—"

"Rub that pussy for me. Make it cum for me." I pulled the curtain across the line to block all view into my cell. Then I pulled my dick out and stroked it. "Let me hear you lick your fingers like it's my dick—"

* * *

I had dozed off after several rounds of phone sex with Val. The cell door opening loudly stirred me awake. I got up and went to the door.

"Carter, you got a visit. Go to screen five."

* * *

My sister's face filled the screen mounted on the wall. She was the female image of myself and I loved her a great deal. "Lin, what's up beautiful?"

"I'm good, brotherman. How are you?"

"I'm great. You?"

53

"Concerned."

"About what?"

"You. And your daughter. The grey-eyed spawn of Ameen—"

"Whoa… whoa… what does Quran—"

"Big brother, have you gone dumb in your older years? How could you ask me what does Ameen's son have to do with anything? I told you that Zin is with him and she's pregnant. You haven't said shit to her about him. She knows the two if you are in cahoots with each other and y'all hid it. I'm quite sure that Zin has grilled him about you. And if she showed me the letter she has, who's to say that she hasn't confronted him with it since his name is in it. And if my instincts are correct, then that means he knows your secret."

"Lin, these visits are monitored so I can't speak freely, but I'm curious. What do you think Quran knows? What secret?"

"What secret? The one about Ameen. Patricia said it in the letter. I told you that."

I was confused completely. "Hey, we gon' end this visit. I'ma holla at you in a few minutes, though. Feel me?" The look on my face spoke volumes.

"Okay, I'll be waiting on your call."

* * *

In my cell, I powered up the cellphone and waited. I wanted to give Linda time to get to her car. Once I was satisfied that enough time had passed, I called her phone.

"Hello?" Linda answered.

"Lin, you told me about the letter that Patricia wrote. You told me that Zin thinks I killed her mother and some other shit that I can't remember, but what does any of that have to do with Quran?"

"You getting early onset dementia, too, I see. I told you the letter says that Patricia said that you ordered Quran and

Dontay to kill her. And that she believed that you knew that she was having an affair with Ameen Bashir. She admitted to being with him at y'all house in bed one night and believed you caught them in bed but hid it. In the letter, she said that you killed Ameen. If Zin has confronted that boy with that letter, he knows that you killed his father. You and I never talked about the situation, but we both know the truth.

"Everybody knew that Ameen had been fucking Patricia Mitchell since she was a kid. Everybody but YOU! I knew how much you loved Patricia so I never said shit, but I knew that eventually, you'd find out. I know how you feel about Ameen. I know how deadly that could turn out once you found out. So, I kept quiet but prayed that Patricia and Ameen were savvy enough to hide their shit from you.

"When Ameen turned up dead on his front porch, I knew what happened. I knew who killed him, without you ever saying a word. Your secret was mine to keep. But now that secret has come back to haunt us. If that boy… Quran… Ameen's son is as vicious as his father, which the streets say he is… how can you not be concerned about him? You don't think he'll kill your ass as soon as you step foot out of that jail?"

There were so many thoughts going through my head that it took me a few minutes to respond to my sister. Everything she had just said was on point. "Do you really think that Zin has confronted Quran with Patricia's letter?"

"I can't confirm or deny, but you know your daughter just as well as I do and if she loves that boy… and I'm sure that she does, Zin has already showed him the letter where her mother implicates him in her murder. She's pregnant by that boy. Zin is a lawyer, curious by nature. If her mother predicted that you wanted her dead and that Quran would be the one to kill her, there's no way in the world that Zin would let that ride. But to be absolutely sure, I'm gonna find out—"

"That's not necessary Lin. I think it's time that me and my daughter had a real long talk."

"And big brother, that talk might come sooner than you think." Linda said.

"Why do you say that?" I asked.

"Because, if I'm not mistaken, Zin is pulling you out today. On a legal visit."

CHAPTER 9

ZIN

Central Treatment Facility (CTF)
1901 E Street S.E.
Jihad walked into the room looking like a twin version of Quran. On his face was a look of concern. He sat down in the chair across the table from me. Without any pleasantries, Jihad leaned into me and asked, "Have you talked to my brother?"

"Well, hello to you too, Jihad. I'm fine. Thanks for asking. And I didn't have other things to do better than dropping everything and running over here to see you. Upon request, I might add. A very persistent request. How are you today?"

"I'm good, Zin," Jihad sighed, contrite. "Sorry. Forgive me for being rude. I'm not myself. As you can see, I'm a little stressed out."

"That seems to be affecting everybody lately. Apology accepted, though. And yes, I have talked to Quran."

"Greg Gamble has our cells bugged. Mine and Dave's. Can he do that?"

I shook my head. "Technically, no. There has to be a court ordered request signed by a judge, granting Gamble permission to put a listening device in your cell and in David's cell. And since I'm David's lawyer, I'm one hundred percent certain that no judge gave Greg Gamble permission to bug those cells. He did that on his own, but he had help. Serious help. Gamble is in violation and nothing on those devices can be used against you or David—"

"What about Quran? What about Sean Branch? Do you know Sean?"

"No, but why are you so concerned about Sean Branch? Do you know Sean?"

Jihad's body sagged before my eyes. "Not like that. But my stupid ass… I had no clue that anything remotely close to bugging a cell was even possible and I was running… Dave asked me some questions about shit that nobody could talk about over the phone and I answered them. I told him some shit that Que and Sean did together. Shit that I had no business repeating. To nobody. Shit about some murders. I fucked up, Zin. Bad. if Quran doesn't kill me, Sean Branch surely will." Jihad laid his head on the table and shook it back and forth. "Can't believe I did that stupid ass shit. Now, I'm fucked."

"Quran told me about the cells being bugged. I can't lie and say that he's not pissed."

"See what I mean? They gon' kill me." Jihad repeated over and over.

My heart broke for Jihad. "If it makes you feel any better, Quran's anger is more or less directed at Gamble, not you."

"Do you know how Quran even knows… How did he find out that the cells were bugged?"

"Sean Branch told him. Apparently, Sean has an inside source who tipped him off. He contacted Quran and told him." I leaned across the table to get closer to Jihad.

"Your brother is very pissed about the bugged cells. Don't ever repeat this… He wants to kill Gamble."

Jihad looked up at me. "What? He really said that? That says a lot. He ain't gon' stop there. He gon' kill me and Dave, too."

"Stop fuckin' saying that, Jihad. Quran is not going to kill you."

"If he don't, Sean Branch is for sure. If Sean's source knows about the bugs, they know about what was said. The source has to know that I ran my mouth about Sean. That's why the source contacted him. Whatever the source told him concerned Sean enough to get at Quran and tell him. That made b ruh send messages to me and Dave and tell us to stop running our mouths about shit in the cells because they are bugged. With all the shit Sean got going on right now, he wouldn't have reached out to Bruh unless it was serious shit. That's how I know that I'm dead meat. Bruh is gonna kill me just like he did Tabu. Watch!"

"Quran is not going to kill you, Jihad. You're all he has left. Family wise. He knows that and you know that. That's why he's focused on getting rid of Gamble. Have you talked to Charles Daum lately?"

"Now, why? Should I talk to him? Call him or something?"

"No. He probably doesn't know about the cells being bugged. Let's keep it like that. The less people who know, the better. Just sit tight and be cool. Don't talk on any phones... cellphones or jail phones and stop talking to David about street shit. I'll come back and see you in a few days after I've talked to Quran again. And remember what I said... Don't tell anyone about Quran wanting to kill Gamble!"

* * *

The look of concern on David Battle's face matched the one on Jihad's face moments ago. "Hey, you heard about the bugged cells, huh?"

I nodded. "Greg Gamble is out of pocket. Way out of pocket. I want to approach him about it but I can't. That exposes our hand."

"So, what do we do about it?"

"Nothing."

"Nothing?"

"Nothing. Just be more careful. Don't say shit about shit in your cell or in Jihad's. Nothing on those devices can hurt you—"

"But... Jihad admitted to me that him and Que killed Tommy, Yolanda, Yolanda's uncle Mann and Khitab. Doesn't that give him enough ammo to reopen my case and prove that I had the witnesses against me killed?"

"Look, that was some stupid as shit you did. Discuss your dismissed case in the cell. It was careless and reckless. But it's done and now Gamble knows that he was right. His office was right when they accused you of orchestrating the deaths of those witnesses. That's bad, but not all bad. Not one word of it. Planting those bugs was illegal. He could go to jail for it. I knew it. He knows it. He'll never let those audios see the light of day. Those bugs violate your fourth and sixth constitutional rights. He has the tapes, bugs, audio... or whatever, but he can't use them. Not against you at all. But—"

"But What?"

"Quran says that Gamble is using what he heard to point all the wrong people in the right directions. So, what effect those bugs have on Quran and Sean remains to be seen."

"Jay was right. This shit is gonna get the both of us killed." David muttered.

"And just like I told him moments ago, nobody's getting killed." I replied. "That's what you say, but you don't know Quran Bashir like I know him."

* * *

Across the street...
Central Detention facility (D.C. Jail)
1901 D Street S.E.

"Ronald, your case has been moved to federal court because the guy you pistol whipped and robbed snitched, He says you assaulted him on East Capitol Street near the entrance to RFK Stadium. And unfortunately, that entire tract of land is owned by the federal government. It's federal land."

"Federal Land?" Ronald English exclaimed. "How the fuck is East Capital Street federal land? In Southwest D.C.?"

"It's federal land. Southeast or no Southeast. It's federal. I checked"

"That ain't proper, Ms. Carter. They should have to tell a nigga shit like that."

"They do, Ronald. In school. I learned that but forget about it," I replied. "So, here's where we are. Your base offense level is 26. In your case the B (4) B1 enhancement applies—"

"Before B what? An enhancement? Why do I get an enhancement?"

"The firearm that was fired in your possession AFTER the robbery/assault had scratched off serial numbers." I opened the book in front of me and found the chapter that addressed altered and obliterated serial numbers means a serial number of a firearm that has been changed, modified, affected, defaced, scratched, erased or replaced to make the original information less accessible. Even if such information remains legible. The cumulative offense lever 29. Except if subsection (b) 3A applies. Subsection (b) 3A does not apply to you, Ronald, so your base offense level becomes 29—"

"I never checked no gun for no scratched off serial numbers. I didn't know that the serial numbers were altered or whatever." Ronald argued.

I continued reading. "Subsection B (4) b1 applies regardless of whether the defendant knew or had reason to believe that the firearm was stolen or had an obliterated serial number. We can't get around the enhancement. This is what you signed up for when you made the conscious decision to do what you did to the victim—"

"I should've killed his bitch ass. Rat, bitch ass nigga."
Ronald said and smacked his forehead. "I went against my
first instinct and let T-Rell live. After all the telling he did on
my first cast, I let him make it. This case is supposed to be a
murder case. The fact that I just came home after I won my
appeal is the only reason Terrell Hargrave ain't dead. He
wasn't playing the hood after he snitched on me in 2007.
Ain't nobody been seeing him. As soon as I come home, his
fat bitch ass wanna make an appearance. One of my men saw
him in the area... on foot at that. By the time I got close, his
ass was all the way down by the stadium. I was so mad that
I wanted to crush him, but I didn't. I just pistol whipped him
and went in all his pockets. Stupid ass me. I left the rat
breathing to finger me again. Stupid ass me... fuck!"

Ronald English was visibly upset. I ignored his spontaneous
outburst. "Next is your criminal history score—"

"Choo, please don't kill me! Choo, please...! Don't kill
me, slim! That's what his hot bitch ass said to me as I stood
over him." Ronald said, with a faraway look in his eyes. As
if he was reliving the moment. He shook his head vigorously
then looked over at me. "I should've killed his ass, Ms.
Carter. I fucked up again. I swear I did."

"You had two prior felonies before this one, so that gives
you six points. One felony conviction equals three points.
Six criminal history points puts you in category three." I
turned the chart that I had in front of me around for Ronald
to see it. "With a base offense level of 29 and a criminal
history category of three, that puts your sentencing exposure
at 92 to 115 months. If you accept the plea that the
government has extended, you get a three level reduction to
level 26. Your guideline range becomes 63 to 78 months. I'll
argue for the low end... the 63 months. That's five years and
three months—"

"With good time, I'm looking at four and a half years. I'm
forty four years old, I'll be home before I'm 50. Tell the
government, I'll take the cop to 63 months. Try to get them

to cap it at 63. I came home from Canaan USP. I hope the feds send me back there—"

"Canaan USP? You came home from Canaan?" I asked.

Ronald nodded. "Yeah, I was there for about five years. Why?"

"Because my father is there. Well... not right now, he's here at the jail on a writ. But he's been at Canaan for years too."

"Who's your father, Ms. Carter?"

"Michael Carter."

A bright smile crossed Ronald's face. "Get the fuck outta here! Mike Carter is your father?"

It was my turn to smile. Ronald's exuberance was contagious. "Yeah, that's my dad."

"Everybody knows Mike Carter. I heard that he was back on appeal. I wonder what block he's in."

"He's in Southwest Two."

"That's what's up. I'm tryna holla at him. Since he get everybody's rats killed, I need to get him to send somebody at my rat. Real talk. Mike be getting shit wacked. And he ran up a bog by doing that shit. If I gotta do almost five years, I might as well do it knowing that Terrell Hargrave is dead. Damn... Michael-fuckin'-Carter is at this jail. Him getting his men n'em to smoke T-Rell is meant to be—"

* * *

"Hi, I need to see another client, please. My last one."

The male, African CO looked up from his book he read from inside the bubble. "Who do you need, Ms. Carter?"

"Michael Carter. D.C. number 253-082. Southwest Two unit."

"I'm calling for him right now. Have a seat in the lawyer's room."

* * *

63

"Hey Dad." I said as I stood up and extended my hand to my father. "This is a professional visit so we can't hug. You look good."

My father shook my hand and took a seat across the table from me before responding. "Gotcha, baby girl. I can respect that. As for my looks, prison preserves a good man. How are you? You look good as well. Seems like you're glowing."

"It's the baby, Dad. This baby is changing everything about me."

"I think I'm gonna enjoy being a Granddad."

"Glad to hear it. First things first, I heard through the grapevine that judge Hamilton is going to overturn your conviction—"

"Thank God. Thank you. Thank you. Thank you," my father repeated over and over again.

"Didn't know you were religious," I commented once my father got quiet.

"I'm not, but I felt the need to give thanks to something or somebody. Even if the universe or the stars that shine. Maybe it was for the ancestors. They had some kinda God in them to be able to survive all that shit they survived. My sacrifice in jail pales in comparison."

"Your sacrifice?"

"Yeah. That's what I call it."

"It's your sacrifice because you're innocent, right?"

"Exactly."

"And you always said you were innocent."

"I did."

"So, why didn't you ever just come out and say who really killed Dontay Samuels?"

"What? What do you mean? Say what to who?"

"I came here today to clear the air with you. The video visits weren't a good avenue to do that. I could only say certain things and you could only say certain things. With the video visits being monitored and recorded and all. This conversation we are about to have is long overdue."

"You just said that word around the grapevine is that the judge is gonna overturn my conviction. If he does that I can be released until the government decides if they wanna retry me, right?"

"Right."

"So, why couldn't this conversation wait until I'm a free man?"

"Let's just say it couldn't wait. Not a moment longer for me. I don't know exactly when you'll be free. I need answers to my questions and I need them now. Depending on how this conversation goes, it dictates if you even have a daughter when you're freed. And whether or not you'll ever get to see this baby—"

"Zin, are your serious right now?" My father asked with conviction.

"Deadly serious, Dad. Deathly. And speaking of death, before you answer any questions, I have something for you to read. I extracted a copy of my mother's letter from my purse and pushed it across the table to my father. "Read it." I kept my eyes glued to my father's face as he read the letter.

"So, this is the infamous letter that I've been hearing about?"

"Do you think it's written by someone other than my mother?"

"Of course not. It's Patricia's handwriting all day. I'm sure that she wrote this. Why didn't you come to me first when you got this" And where exactly did you get this anyway?"

"Doesn't matter where I got it from, Dad, I got it. And coming to you with the letter first, what difference would that have made?"

"It would have made a difference. Would've showed your confidence in me. Would've told me that you didn't believe—"

"Before you go any further, Dad, please understand that you're under oath. My oath. An oath that binds you to tell the truth or lose it all. Me, this baby, everything. And before you speak, remember that I'm a lawyer. I've done my own investigations and research. You are the fourth person to read that letter by design. I know way more than you think I know...!"

"From who? Delores Samuels? Your aunt Linda? From Quran Bashir?"

"Moments ago, you said, "So this is the infamous letter that I've been hearing about?" You've been talking to someone. Quran or Aunt Linda. That's cool, though. The truth is the truth and it needs no support. So, I'll start here. Why did you lie to me about Quran?"

"For the same reasons that you did."

"For the same reasons I did what?"

"Lied about him. About you being with Quran and not Jermaine." My blood pressure soared. I laughed despite my anger building. "I never lied to you about anybody. I just never told you about me and Jermaine breaking up and me hooking up with Quran. You lied about him."

"He wasn't for you, Zin. I wanted to protect you from him. From dudes like him. Quran Bashir is for the streets, not you—"

"You lied to me about Quran before we ever hooked up. He was from the area that you grew up in. He was friends with people you knew. I asked you about him and you lied. Told me that you didn't know him! Why?"

"I lied for reasons you will never understand, Zin."

"Liar. The entire jig is up and still you sit in front of me and lie. You lied to me about Quran to keep your secret, Dad. Or should I say secrets, plural. The chances of me even meeting Quran was slim and none to you. But a chance meeting while I was looking for a witness to interview in Sheridon Terrace increased those odds. You lied about knowing Quran because you didn't want me to find out the truth."

"The truth?" My father repeated. "What truth? What's in that letter?"

I nodded. "That, too, but I'm talking about the fact that you knew that Dontay Samuels didn't kill my mother, despite you letting me believe that for almost twenty years. You knew that Quran Bashir killed Dontay Samuels because you told him to. Dontay had begun to talk too much about things that you wanted to keep hidden. So, you made his best friend kill him. While you watched from your car. You lied about Greg Gamble.

"I asked you specifically when I visited you in Canaan, did you know Greg Gamble before he prosecuted you at trial. You looked me right in my face and lied. I could sense that there was some sort of history between the two of you, that's why I asked you that in the first place. You left me in the blind, but it's cool. I guess telling me the history about you and Gamble would've opened Pandora's box and you wanted to keep it closed. Right?"

My father said nothing.

"Telling me about Gamble, about how you ordered his brother's death, because of drug debt and sent Sean Branch to do it would have been too much information for my ears. Because then you'd have to tell me that after you had Sean kill Gamble's brother, that you later ordered a young Quran to kill his sister Cindy. Oh.. and speaking of a young Quran, you didn't care to mention that you knew Quran, because then you'd have to tell me about your relationship with his father Ameen. A man that I vaguely remember. Didn't want to go down that rabbit hole, huh, Dad? Didn't want to admit to me that you groomed Ameen Bashir's son to kill people for you. Because that would lead to the truth about Dontay. Dontay Samuels also killed people for you, right? You never mentioned that to me, Dad. Never told me that you knew him. Never told me that you used to have sex with his Mom—"

"Delores told you that?"

"Does it matter? It's the truth, right? The woman was married but separated and strung out on drugs. You took advantage of her situation and sexed her whenever Dontay wasn't around. Or did Dontay know that you was sexing his mother? Naw, probably not. So, you never told me about Gamble and his vendetta against you, Sean Branch, the Bashir family and who else? Oh... ME! Greg Gamble wants to ruin my career because of his beef with you, and you thought it was a good idea to leave me clueless." I shook my head as I tried to gauge my father's demeanor.

His face was expressionless.

"I thought by going to college and law school, that I could get the best education possible, but I was wrong. The education that I've got over the last year is better than any I've gained my entire life. In the last year I've learned that Jermaine Mendenhall secretly craved fat, white bitches and that he was never really the man for me. I learned that betrayal comes in all forms. Even in the form of your boss wanting your mom. I learned that I could and needed to be my own boss. I learned that betrayal comes in the form of a brother. I learned that as much as you, Aunt Linda and the world tried to shield me from real life, life in Southeast D.C., that I would be drawn back there anyway. I learned that I never really knew what love was until I met my soulmate—"

"Your soulmate? I hope—"

"Dammit, let me finish. I learned that I could watch a man die in front of me and feel absolutely nothing about it. I learned how to compartmentalize. I learned a lot about my family. My Mother's side of the family. I learned that my mother was not the perfect angel that I thought she was. I learned that I could become a mother. I learned that my father has no truth in him—"

"Zin, wait a minute—" my father protested.

"No, Dad, you wait a minute. I learned that my paternity was in question—"

"No, it's not. I am your father. Me! There's no doubt—"

"And that the man I love could possibly be my fuckin' brother—"

"Quran Bashir is not your brother. Now, you're being dramatic!"

"I learned that my mother loved another man besides you. And for that she was killed—"

"That's not true, Zin. You have to understand—"

"Understand what, Dad? That you found out about Ameen Bashir and Mom and got jealous despite the fact you were fucking his wife? Understand what, Dad? That I stood in an abandoned building on Douglas Road and watched Quran Bashir kill his own brother? Do you deny that Bashir's youngest son was your child? Huh? Answer that, Dad!" Again, my father remained silent. His reticence confirming the truth. "I learned that my father went away on a trip, only to return and find my mother in bed with another man. A man that she'd been secretly seeing since she was twelve years old. I learned that my father felt scorned and that he—"

"Don't say it, Zin...please don't say it!"

"...exacted his revenge by killing Ameer Bashir's first and then my mother. You killed my mother, Dad!"

"Zin, stop it!" My father bellowed and rose from his seat. "Stop this shit! Stop saying shit like that! Just because Delores says that and Quran probably said that, doesn't make it true! Nobody knows—"

"The letter says it, Dad. Read it again. Look at it. My mother said it. She predicted her own death. It's right there in her own handwriting." I snatched up the cop of my mother's letter that my father held moments ago. Then I stood up. "Here, read the letter again."

"I don't need to read it again. I know what it says."

"So, admit it Dad. Be a man and tell your daughter the truth for once. Be the man that I always thought you was. Come clean, Dad. Cleanse your soul. Speak your truth. Tell me what made you do all the shit you've done. Make me understand all the moves you've made. All the secrets you've kept. All the lies you've told. Tell me that everything I just said is the truth. Say it!'

My father, dressed in the orange two-piece uniform, that was every inmate in the jail was required to wear, didn't say a word to me. He simply turned, walked over to the visiting room door, opened it and left.

With the door ajar, I could hear him bang on the glass to get the C.O. in the bubble's attention.

"Get me the fuck outta here! I'm ready to go back to my block!"

Riveted to my spot, I could only watch as the steel door that led to the inside of the D.C. jail opened and my father's retreating figure disappeared from view.

CHAPTER 10

MIKE CARTER

"Get me the fuck outta here! I'm ready to go back to my block!"

I never looked back at Zin. I let the look on her face when I left the lawyer's room be the look I remembered as I turned away. I could see the hurt in her expression. I could see the accusation, the betrayal, the pain, the desire for answers. I could see it all in my daughter's face. Zin wanted answers to questions that I couldn't answer. She wanted unspoken truths that I could speak. I walked slowly through the hallway of the D.C. jail and I knew the dynamic of my relationship with my only living child had changed. I thought about everything that Zin had said as anger creeped into my soul. The extent of Zin's knowledge of the past was great. Her words, all facts. Words that had been given to her by people whom I trusted to never speak such truths. Quran Bashir, Sean Branch, Linda Carter... I never factored into the equation that out of the shadows would come Delores Samuels. She was the X Factor that I never saw coming.

I thought about all the things that Delores must have said to Zin and cringed inside. I thought about Zin confronting Quran and in his desire to keep Zin and his unborn child close, I heard his voice. I heard him admitting to things that shouldn't have been admitted to. As I reached the Southwest

Two housing unit, I understood now more than ever that my relationships with Sean and Quran had also changed.

I understood that the letter that Zin carried around was a smoking gun that connected me on every level. I overstood that Quran and Sean Branch were no longer allies. I overstood that two of D.C.'s most illustrious killers were now my enemies. I handed my hall pass to the C.O. in the bubble and waited for the steel door to open that led into the unit.

I heard my name called out a couple times, but I ignored the voices. On the bottom tier, I went straight for my cell. As I approached it, the cell door slid open. I walked into the cell and leaned up against the concrete wall across from my bunk. The cell door closed slowly. I closed my eyes and listened to the sound of my daughter's voice in my head…

"...*the man I love could possibly be my fuckin' brother*—"

"*Quran Bashir is not your brother. Now, you're being dramatic!*"

"*I learned that my mother loved another man besides you. And for that she was killed*—"

The letter that Patricia had written materialized in my head. Suddenly, I could see every line, every sentence, every word. Hearing about the letter was one thing. Seeing it and reading it was another. I could imagine my wife writing that letter. It was as if I could hear her voice talking— speaking her truths. I rubbed my eyes and then rubbed the spot above both my temples.

How in the hell had that letter surfaced? How had it survived almost two decades? Where had Zin gotten the letter from? Those questions and more swirled around in my head with no answers to be had. Again, my anger threatened to boil over. I remembered the first thing that Zin had told me. That the grapevine was abuzz with talk that the case was about to be overturned. I could hear Jon Zucker's voice in my head.

"If the court decides to overturn the conviction, you're coming home, Mike. This judge… Bruce Hamilton, will definitely release you into some type of supervision. I promise you that. The moment the judge mouths the order to overturn, hour after that, you'll be a free man—"

Being a free man meant that I'd become a real target. A target that my enemies could get to easily with the right information. My instincts drove my survival mode into overdrive. The situation I was now in with Zin had to be fixed, but dealing with my enemies would have to come first. I went to my spot in the cell and pulled out my cellphone. Once the phone was powered on, I dialed a number.

"Yo—" a man answered on the second ring.

"Youngin, it's me." I said into the phone.

"Mike?"

"The one and only. Listen, you ready to get some real paper?"

"You already know. What's the 411?"

"I got a hundred bands for you. One fifty if you act quickly."

"One fifty? Big homie, I'll fly to Rome and body the Pope for one fifty. Who I gotta go see to get that kinda bread?"

"It's not one person, youngin. It's two. I need them both *gone* in the next day or two. You think you can do that?"

"You muthafuckin' right. Gimme the two names and I'm on it today."

"Good. The two people I need dead are Quran Bashir and Sean Branch."

"Grey eyed Que and Teflon? You gotta be kidding?"

"Does it sound like I'm kidding?"

"Damn! Say less, big homie. I'm on it. Send me any info that'll be helpful and I'm on the clock."

"I'm texting it to you as we speak—"

CHAPTER 11

SUSAN ROSENTHAL

United States Attorney's Office
555 4th St. N.W.
"Marquee Venable committed the murder when he was sixteen years old. Better yet, he never committed the murder he's been in prison almost fifteen years for. His only crime is being guilty of honoring the street code by never revealing who really killed the victim that day. "Laura Esch argued. "And research has shown that brain development continues until the mid-twenties on average. Potentially contributing to impulsive behavior and reward seeking action—"

"Come on, Laura, either Venable committed the murder or he didn't. You can't have it both ways. He didn't do it, but he did it because his brain hadn't fully developed. And since you weren't there, research has also shown a correlation between age and rearrest rates, with younger individuals being re-arrested at higher rates and reoffending more often after release from prison, than older individuals. So, the question to me is, do I want an older Marquee Venable to be released back into the community after serving a minimal amount of the fifty years he was sentenced to and my answer is no—"

"Susan, certain sentences for offenses committed prior to age eighteen are considered in the calculation of a defendant's criminal history score. The guidelines specifically distinguish now between an adult sentence and a juvenile adjudication. That wasn't the case back in 2000 when Marquee Venable was sentenced—"

"Laura, I don't give two fucks about the argument you're trying to present on behalf of your client. I am going to vigorously oppose Marquee Venable's release on appeal. So, in other words, no deal. Excuse my French. If you don't have anything else for me, I'm going to conclude this meeting."

Laura Esch's partner, Mitch Lawlor spoke up next. "I've got two more names for you. Franklin Hunter and Parvis Knighton."

I pulled my laptop out and put the two names into our system. Franklin Hunter was a thief and scammer, whose social media accounts aided in his downfall. Parvis Knighton was a violent offender, currently charged with murder. "Talk to me."

"I need a Sweet cop for Hunter and for that I'll give you Knighton on a plate." Mitchell Lawlor said.

"On a plate? We already have enough to convict Knighton."

"Come on, Susan, you know exactly what I mean. Either I'll convince Knights to cop to one thing, and you can smoke him, or we'll go to trial, and I'll sell him out for you. Throw his defense into the blender."

"You'd agree to do that to save Hunter?" I asked incredulously. Still reading the info on Franklin Hunter. He was a suspect in several smash and grab robberies of jewelry stores in the DMV area.

Mitch nodded. "Yes. I kinda owe the kid, Sue. I helped the guys who killed his father to get off at trial. That case haunted me for a lot of different reasons. When I was given Franklin Hunter's case by the court, I felt that it was divine intervention. A way for me to atone for my sins of the past—"

"You are a defense lawyer, Mitch; you have too many sins to atone for. All the criminals that you've helped to put back on the streets. Why the attack of conscience in this case?"

"I just don't want to see the kid get killed in the federal Bureau of Prisons. And that's exactly what's going to happen if he goes there. His co-defendants are killers. Real unsavory characters. When Franklin, nicknamed 'Gino' after his father, was arrested he foolishly interviewed with FBI agents. He did two things at that debriefing session. He said… on camera… and I quote, 'I'll tell y'all whatever you want to know if y'all let me go home on the GPS box.' Then he was shown a photo array with several of his co-defendants included, even a picture of his blood brother.

"His response to seeing the photo array was, and again I quote, 'This is everybody. Y'all got everybody involved in the robberies, so why do you want me?' His co-defendants were shown copies of that debriefing and word spread quickly throughout the prison system that Lil Gino is a rat. D.C. jail prison officials intercepted kites where people called for his life to be taken. They have recorded jail calls where people are discussing killing Franklin Hunter—"

"Where is Hunter now?" I asked.

"I got a judge to sign an immediate injunction that authorized the U. S. Marshalls to move him out of the D.C. jail. Hunter is now at Rappahannock Regional jail in Stafford, Virginia for his own safety."

"Is Franklin Hunter willing to testify against… let me see." I looked at my laptop. "William Hunter, Robert Shefield and the remaining two co-defendants who haven't copped yet?"

"I'm sure he will."

"Okay, Mitch, I'm intrigued. You give us Parvis Knighton… 'on a plate' as you say, and get Hunter to roll over on his brother and co-defendants, if I give him a Sweet Deal. I like it. Let's do it."

* * *

Tabitha Kearney reminded me of Jennifer Hudson, but prettier. She walked into my office and plopped her ample butt down into one of the chairs that lined the wall. She closed her eyes and leaned her head back to rest on the wall. Minutes passed without her saying a word.

"Uh… hello to you too, Tabitha. Can I help you, my dear?" I said a little irritated by the unannounced intrusion.

"Sorry, Sue," Tabitha responded as she opened her eyes. "I needed to get away for a while. My office can get like Grand Central Station sometimes. And," Tabitha removed one of her heels and rubbed her foot, "everybody is getting on my last good nerve. Chris in Appellate, Ian McNeely, Dan Horowitz, Davin York, Ann, Ari and Greg. It seems like I been running all day. Superior Court, District Court, back to Superior Court. I'm tired, I'm hungry, cramping and PMS'ing. So, pardon my intrusion, but at the moment, you're my only respite. Seems to me folks want to avoid you like Smallpox, so I know that your office wouldn't be crowded."

"I'm not sure if I should be offended or happy to hear that. But take as long as you need, lady. I'm just finishing up a motion to include the 2013 Prince George's County traffic stop and arrest of Antonio Johnson into evidence in case he decides to go to trial on his current charges. Judge Potter is a stickler for details and I plan to give him all the details he needs. After this, I'ma call it a day."

"I wish I could call it a day too, but tonight is my late night. I've got case files stacked a foot high, calls to make and deadlines to meet. And speaking of Smallpox, have you heard anything from OAG or the OPR yet?"

"Not a word, but I heard that Greg has. His days as a United States Attorney are numbered, I think and I'm not quite sure how I feel about it."

Tabitha took her time putting her red bottomed heel back on before pulling off the other. After rubbing her foot for a while, she said, "In the words of my ancestors, 'It don't make me no never mind if he goes or stays.' As long as the next boss is promoted from within, I'm good. I figure that will either be, Ari Weinstein, Ann Sloan or you who will end up sitting on that throne. Damn, these puppies are really killing me. Christian Louboutins are pricey and they look good, but they are rough on pretty feet. I need a pedicure, a foot massage and a happy ending—"

Laughter escaped my mouth. "A happy ending? Are you serious? Didn't you just say that you were PMS'ing?"

"Sue, happy endings feel better when you're on your menstrual. You didn't know that?"

"Uh... never heard of that, lady. You just made that up."

"I didn't make it up. Maybe it's only for black women though."

"Maybe. All I know is that I have never done anything sexual while Mother Nature was in town."

"Honey," Tabitha continued, "in Cosmopolitan magazine they call it 'running a red light'. Get your ass in the shower and get dicked down or do the honors yourself and act like its just water running down your leg. I'm telling you, Sue... best fucking orgasm in the world."

Shaking my head, I endeavored to clear it of the images that Tabitha conjured up. "How did we go from work, Greg Gamble successors and Smallpox to period sex and happy endings?"

Tabitha put her heel back on, then slowly stood up. "That's how life is sometimes. You want apples or cherries, but the world gives you lemons. You get hungry and want food, but then you realize that it's your thirst that needs to be quenched. Then you figure out that that's what the lemons were for. Lemonade will always cure your thirst. When you leave tonight, drive safe."

"What?" I said to myself and laughed. I didn't understand a word of what the woman had just said.

* * *

As I exited the building where I worked, I had to stop and button my coat to the top button to ward off the cold that threatened to freeze me. I walked down fourth street and crossed Indiana Avenue. A familiar vehicle approached. The dark colored Jaguar sedan came to a complete stop in front of me and the passenger side window lowered. I recognized the face that appeared and I couldn't repress the smile that crept across my face. "Yes, Benito?"

"Good evening, Susan, Carlos requires your presence." Benito Alvarez said. His words more a command than a request. "He sent me to get you."

I pulled my cellphone out of my coat pocket and looked at it. There were no missed calls. Why didn't he just call—"

Benito stepped out of the car and held the car door open. "You'll have to ask him when you see him, chica. Let's not keep him waiting. Mario, 3122 Goldstone Village Drive."

I needed to get home. I was tired, hungry and in need of a drink, but as always, whenever Carlos Trinidad beckoned, I answered. I walked slowly to the Jaguar and climbed into the backseat.

* * *

After reading the signs on the road, I ascertained that I was in Brandywine, MD. My inner voice told me that there were only two people who I knew of that lived in the Washington D.C. suburb. I was led to a red brick Colonial style house. One of Carlos' men that I recognized immediately, opened the door of the home. I entered the house and the living room. One person in each chair, restrained at the ankles and wrists. The two people were fully clothed, the one closest to where I now stood was dressed in hospital scrubs and colorful crocks. A dark hood covered the two peoples faces. But I had an idea who the people were.

Carlos eyed me from the moment I walked into the house until I stood near the two chairs. His eyes revealed nothing. My eyes revealed curiosity and questions. Carlos' jacket was off. He stood near the house's kitchen with his shirt sleeve rolled up to the elbows. Again, I eyed the captives.

"Carlos, why am I here?"

Carlos walked closer to me. He smiled. "Why are you here?" Carlos repeated and sat down on one of the two couches in the living room. "Let me tell you why you are here. I have always tried to shield you from the dark side of my business. I did that for good reasons. But recently you decided to step into the light. To cross that well-crafted, fine line between good and bad, darkness and light. Since you decided to do—"

The tone in Carlos' voice was making me nervous. The expression on his face as he spoke was one that I'd never seen. "Wait... I'm lost. What decision did I make? I have no clue as to what you're talking about. Darkness and light. What line have I crossed?"

"The line you crossed, Susan, is the one that was obliterated the day you ordered me to kill for you. Then you did it again the day you decided that Maryann Settles needed to die to prevent her from testifying at that hearing—"

"There's been a mistake, Carlos. I never really meant... I was upset—"

"There's been no mistakes, Susan." Carlos said and rose from his seat. He walked up to me and put his fingers to my lips to quiet me. "You wanted me to kill for you. You demanded that I remove the obstacles from your path. You have been obediently by my side for too many years to count. You've helped my organization in ways that I can never repay you for. You have been an asset to me and I can never thank you enough for your service. Your loyalty. But tonight is different. I need a different kind of showing of your loyalty. Tonight, I require a blood sacrifice from you. I need you to kill for me."

Tears formed in my eyes and fell. I grabbed Carlos' fingers and moved them from my lips. "Carlos… I can't! I can't do that! I can't kill… I… I'm not you! I'm not one of your men!"

"You can't kill." Carlos turned to Benito Alvarez and said, "She can't kill."

Benito Alvarez left the room and returned moments later walking a man into the room. The man was dressed in a blue pinstriped suit, and wore a hood over his head. His arms were pulled to the back of him. His wrists were bound together. I recognized the shoes the man wore. They were the Bruno Maglia wing tipped leather shoes that I'd paid for in Paris a couple of years ago. The tailored blue suit was made by Donatella Versace herself.

"Carlos…please don't do this!" I cried out. "Leave my husband out of this! He has nothing to do with anything I do!"

"One day soon, Susan, you will become the United States Attorney for the District of Columbia. And I need assurances that once you've grown larger in stature, that you won't forget the loyalty we've forged over the years. The golden haired beauty can never forget the beast who has helped her along the way. Your husband's ears are plugged under the hood. He has no idea where he is or who has taken him from his car. If you love him you will honor my request and kill for me. Once you done what I am requesting, he will be drugged lightly and taken to your home. Unharmed. He will go to sleep and remember nothing. Your secrets, our secrets will be safe—"

"I can't kill—"

"Susan, your husband's ears are plugged, but the two people sitting in those chairs are not. They can hear everything we've just said. You've said my name and I've said yours. They cannot be allowed to live. To tell their story of what happened here. They know who you are. They know who I am. You asked me to have them killed—"

"No! No…No…No… Carlos, please don't do this!" I begged.

"Enrique, please give Susan your gun." Carlos demanded softly. As he pulled a handgun from his shoulder holster. He walked over to me and held the gun out for me to take it.

When I hesitated, Carlos walked over to Grant's hooded figure. He put the gun to Grant's head. "Take the gun, Susan. Kill both people sitting in those chairs or your husband dies. Who gets to live tonight, Susan? Maryann Settles and her husband Christopher? Or *your* husband Grant? You have two minutes to decide."

"Carlos… no!" I cried.

"One minute, Susan. Fifty-nine seconds. Fifty-eight—"

I grabbed the gun from Enrique's outstretched hand. I walked over to the two chairs.

"Fifty-five seconds… fifty-four… fifty-three—"

Quickly, I decided to save my husband from imminent death. I crossed the room and pointed the gun at the first hooded person in the chair. It was Maryann Settles. I recognized her shoes. The multicolored Crocks. I inhaled then exhaled. Closed my eyes and pulled the trigger…

CHAPTER 12

QURAN

"Jihad thinks that you're going to kill him."

"He knows he fucked up, but I'm not gonna kill him and he knows that."

"Well, David thinks the same thing. He said it with the same look on his face that Jihad had. They both really believe that, Quran. You got both of them grown ass thugs scared as shit. Who are you, for real?"

"Stop what you doing, Zin." I said and laughed to break the tension. "Them niggas just being dramatic. And we been through this already. You asked me that same question when we first started fuckin' with each other. Besides all that, you know who I am. And what I am."

"Yeah, I do. And I hate that for you. Who you are and why you are who you are. Knowing that my father is to blame for turning you into the person you are is even more sickening. Would it help if I told you that I'm sorry?"

"Didn't I just tell you to stop what you doing? You don't owe me no apolog—"

"I know that, but baby, you can't deny that my father was a bad influence on you as a kid and as a man. You've been kill… working for him your whole life. Then to add insult to injury, he's been misleading you and lying to you… hell, to both of us our whole lives."

"And you say that he just walked away? Like, real live, just turned around and left the room when you confronted him with what you knew?"

"Yep. He left. Didn't say a word. Just turned and left the room. I couldn't believe it. Shit fucked me up, baby. That man left me there with the shit face. Disrespectful as shit. I thought he would have called to apologize by now, but I haven't heard a word from him. Can you believe it" My muthafucking father. Nigga couldn't even be a man. Couldn't even lie. Couldn't do shit. Couldn't say shit. Tough ass Michael Carter was quiet as shit. I still can't believe it. I mean... I knew that my questions would be hard to answer. I knew that my revelations to him about what I knew would fuck him up, but did I expect him to just bitch up and walk away? Naw, I never expected that. Never saw that coming. Not in a thousand years."

"So, what did you expect him to say? To do?" I asked.

"I expected him to lie some more. I expected him to deny everything. Cry maybe... I don't know what I really expected. I just never expected my father to clam up and roll out. I damn sure didn't expect that. Piece of shit ass. Ugghh... he got me mad as shit just thinking about it again... Oooowwww!"

"What? You aight?"

"Yeah, I'm good. I think the baby doesn't want the food I just ate. I thought he liked weird shit like avocados on crab cakes and fried shrimp with garlic corn and pickles."

I laughed at the food Zin had just named. Thinking about what she said made my stomach turn. "You keep saying 'He'. Who said that the baby is a boy?"

"Damn sure ain't no girl with all the wild shit I been craving. And I can see the baby bump now."

"I been saw it, but I just thought you were bloated and had to shit."

"If I had a dick, this would be where I'd tell you to suck it." Zin replied.

"Well, I'm glad you ain't got one because that would be weird as shit. I got one though and you can suck it for me later."

"I'll think about it." Zin said and yawned. "When are you coming here?"

"Soon, baby, soon. As soon as I'm finished what I'm doing, I'll be there." I said as I glanced out the window of the Genesis.

"Okay, then. I will see you when you get here. I'm about to take a bath."

"Aight, talk to you later. I love you."

"Love you too, Que. Be safe."

"I will. Bye."

Tossing my cellphone into the passenger's seat, I kept my eyes glued to the bistro to my right. La'Shukran Bistro in the 400 block of Morse Street in Northeast was an upscale food spot patronized by politicians, law enforcement and government officials. United States Attorney Greg Gamble sat at a table inside the bistro that I could see from the car. The youngish looking white man that gave me young Christian Slater vibes, seated across from Gamble had just recently walked in and joined him.

"I wonder if this white nigga is his boyfriend" I muttered to myself. I moved closer to get a better look at the couple at the table. Smiling to myself, I said "Yeah… that's his boyfriend." I could tell by the way both men interacted in public. It reminded me of the way Zin and I interacted. "This wild ass nigga… he a fag and got the nerve to be fuckin' with a cracka." *Even more reason to smoke his ass. This is gonna be too easy*, I thought to myself as I leaned back in the spacious driver's seat in the Genesis.

Closing my eyes, I thought about an hour earlier when I found an inconspicuous parking spot near the U.S. Attorney's Office building. I didn't know if Greg Gamble used the front entrance of the 555 when he left for the day or an alternate exit. It turned out that Greg Gamble used the front door. From inside the tinted windowed Genesis, I watched Gamble exiting the building and get into a vehicle . The vehicle's windows were also tinted and I couldn't see it's driver. I followed the Lincoln sedan to a few different stops until Greg Gamble finally exited the car and entered La'Shukran Bistro. Satisfied that I'd be able to do exactly what I wanted to do with Greg Gamble, I pulled away from the curb and left.

"Killing him is going to be too easy."

* * *

In the building where Zin lived, she was only provided with one parking space in the garage, which led me to always have to park blocks away and walk to her condo. To me, that was cool because the walk from my car to her building always gave me extra time with my thoughts. It gave me time to get all my lies straight and to delete incriminating female baggage out of my phone. I sat in the car and deleted the text threads from Kiki Swinson and Halima Ndugu. Along with the calls from my log. I left all the texts from Tomasina because Zin knew that Tomasina was my CTF connect. Tomasina never did messy shit and text about our extracurricular activities.

Exiting the car, I thought about the case that Maryland was trying to build. I reminded myself to go and see Douglas Woods, one of the best criminal defense attorneys that Maryland had ever seen and take him a retainer fee. Just in case. I thought about Tosheka Jennings and almost teared up. Killing Tosheka was by far my biggest regret ever. I walked down the block slowly. I pulled my hat down low over my ears and flipped my collar to keep the cold from entering my coat and chilling my body. The next thought that came to mind was Zin's revelation that her father was probably days away from freedom.

Zin's mother's letter appeared in my head. I could see Patricia Mitchell's words about Mike killing my father. I could also hear Sean Branch's words in my head, The day he told me that he always suspected that Mike Carter killed his best friend, Ameen Bashir. Ameen Bashir. My idol. My best friend ever. My father. My whole world.

As I walked, the animal inside me roared. My anger momentarily rose and my fingers moved on their own. My trigger finger itched to feel a gun inside my hand. A gun that was aimed at Mike Carter's head. I imagined myself killing Mike Carter and thought about how Zin would feel about me actually killing her father. One of our last conversations popped in my head…

"Besides, your crime that day was a lesser crime than what I originally thought whenI first found that letter in my mother's things at the condo. I've known for a while now that my father killed my mother. I guess I just wanted to hear it from you. So, let me ask you this question. After reading that letter, how do you feel about my father now?"

"Different. He was like a father to me. Now, I want to kill him—"

"Well, join the club. But no, actually, I don't wish death on my father. Even after what he did to my mother and so many other people. Even your father. So, no, Quran, you can't kill my father."

"I never said that I was gonna kill your father. I just said that I want to."

"And your wants eventually materialize into you actually doing it. I'm hip to you and you know that. So, let me be completely clear. DO NOT KILL MY FATHER, QURAN! Was that clear enough for you?"

"Crystal clear."

"No misunderstandings, correct?"

"None."

I'm sorry, baby girl. That's a promise that I'm gonna have to break."

CHAPTER 13

DET. BOB MATHIS

700 M. Street N.E.
6:17 a.m.

"What do we have here?" I asked as I approached the plain clothed detectives gathered on M Street near Orleans Place.

Dom Capers, a homicide detective out of Fifth District Station, spoke up. "This poor guy is someone we were all familiar with. He just came home a week ago from a Federal prison in Glenville, West Virgina—"

"FCI Gilmer, I think it's called." Frank Watts added.

"Yeah, right. Thanks, Frank. Anyway, Bob, Michael Stevenson is a piece of shit. He was a creep. Sex offender, carjacker and thief. We sent him to prison about twelve years ago for a charge he caught on West Virginia Avenue nearby. Evidently, he came home and pissed somebody off." Johnny pull back the sheet and let Bob see the victim. The technician from the coroner's office pulled the sheet off of Michael Stevenson's corpse.

"Whew!" I exclaimed.

"Obliterated the entire top of his skull. The shell casings are 7.62's. He was shot in both eyes and several times in his mouth. This one is gonna be messy. Brain matter is gonna be on everything—"

"How the fuck did y'all even identify him. The guy doesn't even look human." Dom laughed, then he reached into his pocket and pulled out an evidence bag. He passed the bag to me. "It's the prison ID. See it? The red cord that says Federal Bureau of Prisons. Got it out of his front pocket along with the EBT card, Social and Birth Certificate—"

"So, this has nothing to do with the Miguel Harris and Dontay Wilks murders, right?"

James Dickey, another homicide detective asked.

"I don't think it does," I responded. "Jontavias Minor talked to us and he didn't mention nothing about this guy as far as I remember."

"This has nothing to do with Miguel Harris and that case, just happened to happen in the same area. What somebody did to Stevenon was passionate. It was personal overkill." Dom Capers stated emphatically. "This kill has a female involved in it or this guy snitched before… or he did some creep shit to someone's kids. Watch what I tell you when the witnesses come forward… if they come forward, we are gonna learn that this murder was about one of four things. His mouth, his dick, money or some creep shit involving someone's woman or kids.'

"Whatever it is, it'll be. I'ma get out of here. Got a few leads on some other cases I need to follow up on. You guys take it easy."

* * *

At my desk, I did my research. I looked up everything I could find on Dorrenda, Von and Renaissance Tyler. I searched our system for info on the dead kid Damien Tyler. But there wasn't much to find. Von Tyler had been deceased for over a decade and the wife, Dorrenda had no run in's with the law. Neither had the daughter, Ren Tyler. But they were both rumored to be natural born killers. I leaned back in my chair and thought about something I had been told days ago.

"Dorrenda Tyler has been on the straight and narrow since Von Tyler was killed. She's working at a hospital

downtown somewhere. I went to the blast site on Decatur Street and encountered her—"

"Hey, Joe?" I said into the phone after it was picked up on the other end.

"Bob, what's up, buddy?" Joe Anastasia replied. "Am I in trouble?"

"Stop what you're doing, Joe. Of course you're not in trouble. I was just wondering whether or not you got any info... contact info on Dorrenda Tyler? I'd really like to talk to her about Sean Branch and see if she knows anything about him. I'm kinda not buying this whole 'We don't have any enemies' thing. Somethings telling me that she might know more than she told you. If Sean knew to go to that house, he had to know that Renaissance Tyler wasn't going to be there. I think Sean... if the culprit who blew up the house and killed Damien Tyler... was Sean Branch, he might've had other motivations besides the ones we know about. I can't find shit in the system on Dorrenda or Renaissance Tyler. Nada. Zilch. Nothing. And I want to interview them both—"

"Without letting on to the fact that we suspect Renaissance of being a female serial killer, right?"

"Right... of course. I'd never reveal our hand unless Ren Tyler reveals hers."

"Let me get back to you and see what I can find on the Tylers." Joe told me.

"Great," I replied. "Hit my line. I'll be waiting."

After disconnecting the call to Joe Anastasia, I made another call.

"What's up, Slim?" Sean Branch answered.

"We need to get together."

"When and where?"

"As soon as possible. You call it."

* * *

IF YOU CROSS ME ONCE 6 | ANTHONY FIELDS

Sean held my iPad and watched the video footage of the burgundy SUV pulling up to the curb outside of the Chipotle restaurant that his daughter worked for at the time of her death.

"How do I enhance the images on the screen?" Sean asked me.

I reached out from the passenger's seat and took hold of the iPad. I enlarged the footage and passed the iPad back to Sean.

"Here," Sean said and leaned over towards me. "See the person get out of the SUV and walk into the Chipotle?"

"Ren Tyler, right?"

Sean shook his head. "No. That's Bionca Clark right there. I watched her at the memorial service for her brother at Stewarts. She must've went into the store to see if Shontay was at work. See how moments later she comes out of the Chipotle and gets back into the passenger side of the Infiniti truck? Bionca Clark and Ren Tyler are together. The sister and the girlfriend. Bionca got in the truck and told Ren Tyler that Shontay was in the store. Then they waited—" Sean's voice tapered off. He fast forwarded the footage. "There's Shontay exiting the Chipotle. That's Ren Tyler getting out of the driver's side of the Infiniti to follow her—" Again Sean paused. He handed the iPad to me and without a word exited the Toyota.

I watched from my seat as Sean dropped to his knees on the sidewalk and covered his head in agony. Turning away, I decided to let the man have his moment uninterrupted, unwitnessed by my eyes. I pulled out my cellphone and found the info I'd gotten from Joe Anastasia. I texted that info to Sean's phone along with other info he'd need. I pulled up the secret recordings I had that was audio of Greg Gamble's recordings from Jihad Bashir's cell at CTF. I texted Sean that recording as well. I remembered the day I secretly recorded the recordings on my cellphone without Greg Gamble knowing.

Sean suddenly got back into the Toyota pick. "Anything else I need to know before I go?"

I told Sean about everything I had just sent to his phone. "Is there anything else that I need to know before I go?" I asked Sean. "Any recent bodies that'll pop up or never be found."

"Other than the ones you already know about, naw. There were a few people on my list that I've decided to come back to later. But I'ma let you know now. I have about four hand grenades left and I'm gonna use 'em. One for Bionca Clark. One for Ren Tyler, and one for either Dorrenda Tyler or Brechelle Clark. The last one, I'ma save for myself. I'm not letting nobody arrest me, Slim. I'm going out with a *Bang*... literally. Just so you know."

"I'm not even gon' try to talk you out of any of that because I know I can't. Call me if you need anything. And stay safe until you can't. I'm out."

* * *

"I need that good shit, good shit."

"Have I ever gave you some bullshit, big dawg?"

"If you wanna stay out of prison, you won't."

"Damn, Bobby, the threats. Cut out the threats."

"You need to cut out all the cut, Petey. Get rid of all your fuckin' Mannitol."

Peter Green laughed. "Mannitol? Nobody uses manny to cut dope no more, Bobby. It's all powdered Creatine, bro." The man said and passed me the sandwich bag full of heroin. He held out his hand palm up. "My money."

It was my turn to laugh. "Your money? Get the fuck out of my car, Petey. And stay out of trouble."

I sat and watched Petey walk back to his corner at Seventh and T Street. Smiling, I surreptitiously took a blow out of the sandwich bag. As the raw dope drained down my throat, I leaned my head back. "Damn, this some good shit."

CHAPTER 14

GREG GAMBLE

"I couldn't find any addresses for either Sean Branch or Quran Bashir." Ian McNeely said. "I talked to my source inside the Metropolitan Police Department. Something. The address they had for Sean Branch is the address in Northeast where his mother killed herself. It's obvious that Sean Branch doesn't live there. I'm sure that his former attorney Zinfindel Carter would have..."

"That bitch won't help us. She'd alert Sean that we're on to him at her first sign of trouble. Fuck her and the hospital that she was born in. I just heard that her father will be a free man again soon. The judge hasn't officially announced his decision, but we all know what Judge Hamilton was going to do. It comes as no surprise to me—"

"Nor I. He's called 'Cut Em Loose' for Christ's sake!"

"Right. What about Bashir? Find any current address for Quran Bashir?"

"Not exactly. But when you put his father Ameen Bashir into the system, an address for Eaton Road comes up. But since Berry Farms is about to be torn down, I'm assuming that address is no good. I took the liberty of running Jihad Bashir's info and another name came up. Khitab Bashir. Quran and Jihad's—"

"Brother. Damn, I forgot all about him since his death… his murder that's connected to the Battle case. What came up for Khitab Bashir?"

"An address on Havard Road in Southeast. 1351 Havard Road. Just so you know, Jihad Bashir's linked to the same address on Havard Road. So, how do you want to play it? On books or off. Send one of our guys off record or get Bob Mathis or one of those guys to go there on record.?'

"Off the books. I have a guy that I can use. Khitab's dead and Jihad's in jail. Do you really think that Quran really lives at that address, too?"

Ian McNeely stood up and fixed his suit jacket. "There's only one way to find out. Send your guy and see."

"I'm on it, Ian. Thanks for everything, pal. You're one of the only friends I have left."

"Speaking of such, you had the appointment to see the Attorney General a few days ago, right?"

I nodded.

"What happened? What did Danielson say?"

"I didn't meet with Danielson. I met with his assistant Brad Shaub."

"Well, what did Shaub say? Anything interesting?" Ian asked.

"Asked me a lot of questions about Michael Carter."

"Just Michael Carter?"

"He asked me about a lot of people—"

Someone knocked loudly on my office door, then it opened. It was Tabitha Kearney.

"Hey, Greg. Hey, Ian." Tabitha said and grabbed the T.V. remote off my desk. "Greg, there's something on the news that I think you need to see." She clicked the wall mounted flat screen T.V. on.

"…Detective Morales, have the names of the victims been released to the public yet?"

"Marie, we just release those names moments ago. The victims have been identified as Christopher Settles and his wife Maryann Settles."

"Thank you, Detective. If you've just tuned in. Prince George's County authorities are investigating the shooting deaths of two people found dead in their home in Brandywine. The victims were reported missing by family members. P.G. police went to the house behind us here to do a wellness check and forced entry into the home. They discovered the bodies of Christopher and Maryann Settles, both dead from apparent gunshot wounds—"

Tabitha clicked the T.V. off. Her eyes and Ian McNeely's eyes bore into mine. I could read the accusatory looks in them. Someone had killed Maryann Settles and her husband. Shit was about to hit the fan, literally.

* * *

The conference room at Triple Nickel was packed to the hilt with lawyers and prosecutors.

"Can something like this blow back and touch all of us here." Devin York asked getting the room's attention.

"How could it?" I replied with conviction. "None of us here had anything to do with what happened to the Settles." I looked around until my eyes found that of Susan Rosenthal. "At least, I know for damn sure I didn't."

Ann Sloan spoke next. "We are all here as public servants. We fuck up from time to time with the way we prosecute cases, but none of us here are murderers. We convict murderers, right?"

"Right," Ian McNeely said. "And other people had motives to get rid of the Settles, I'm sure. Who knows what they were into. I think we're all jumping to surreal conclusions. Sure, there's a slight scandal coming out of our office involving two of our own, but certainly we know that Greg and Susan could not be a part of anything this nefarious. Right?"

"We just learned of this news moments ago. Let's just all go back to our regularly scheduled programs and let the local law enforcement officials do their thing. Ian's right. We're jumping to conclusions. As time goes on, we're all going to learn that Maryann Settles and her husband had some shit going on that none of us know anything about. Let's break on that note." Ari Weinstein said authoritatively.

* * *

Ari Weinstein's suit jacket was off and draped across the arm of one of the chairs in my office. He paced the floor in front of my desk. Suddenly, he stopped. "I just remembered the conversation that you and I had the night we were discussing the Rayful Edmonds motion to reduce sentence. I remember all that shit you told me that night, Greg, but hell, I chalked it all up to paranoia. But now this... this is a lot."

"My days as United States Attorney for the District were already numbered, Ari, I know that, but this situation shortens them—"

"In your harangue that night you blamed Susan. You said that Susan stood to benefit the most with you out of the way. I'm not sure if I agree with that now. That night you essentially accused Susan of orchestrating your political demise. Again, considering how things have progressed, I don't see how she can emerge unscathed from this out of control speeding train that's about to derail. So say you."

I breathed a lengthy sigh. " I don't know, Ari. I still think that bitch has something left up her sleeve. Her and Trinidad, maybe. I changed the narrative, though. I did that. I decided not to let her get away unscathed when her name was removed from Maryann Settles original recounted statements. I got Ian to purposely pinpoint and highlight Susan's role in the scandal. Now, here we are. The both of us persona non grata. It looks bad, but I kinda see the poetic justice in it all."

"I also remember everything you said that night about my dirty laundry and you wanting to see me take over your job…If you lost it. Do you still feel the same way?"

Nodding my head, I said, "I do. Why?"

"Because I never asked you this before, Greg and it never mattered before, but somehow now it does. Is it true?"

"Is what true? That I had something to do with the Settles' murders?" I asked, visibly offended.

"No," Ari replied. "I would never ask that question. And I believe wholeheartedly that the answer to that question is, no. I'm asking about the scandal part. Did you really pay Maryann Settles to perjure herself at Michael Carter's trial? And did Susan really help to facilitate that situation?"

I sat up in my seat completely before answering. "Can you handle the truth, Ari?"

"Come on Greg, we are not on set here. This is not a scene out of the movie 'A Few Good Men' and I'm not Tom Cruise. Neither are you Jack Nicholas."

"I did a lot of things in my past, Ari. Things I'm not proud of. It took a lot to gct mc into this scat. Was it all on the up and up? No. Did I do what I felt needed to be done at the time to accomplish my desired goals? Yes. And getting Michael Maurice Carter off the streets in 1995 was definitely one of my biggest goals—"

"Why?" Ari asked. "Why was that one of your biggest goals?"

"Because Michael Carter ordered the execution of my brother… my big brother, Lonnell. After him, he had my sister Cindy murdered. I'm telling you this for two reasons, Ari. One is simply that you asked and two, is because I want you to understand that I'm no killer and I didn't order the Settles' murders. If I was capable of either of those things, Michael Carter would be dead and not about to be free once Judge Hamilton decides to announce it."

"But, why? There's that question again. Why?"

"Why what? Why did Michael Carter order the deaths of my sister and brother?"

Ari nodded.

"First, my brother. Lonnell was a drug dealer, Ari… sorta like you, but not as large in stature. He moved a lot of cocaine in the eighties and early nineties. Some type of dispute over money made Michael Carter order Sean Branch—"

"Sean Branch? 'Teflon' Sean Branch?"

"Yep. Him. He killed people for Michael Carter. Michael Carter got a young Sean Branch to walk into a Salon owned by my brother and kill him. My older sister Cindy found out that it was Mike Carter who had my brother killed. She wanted revenge. Apparently, she expressed her desires to the wrong person and word got back to Carter. He then sent another child killer to murder my sister. I was in school back then… when both murders happened. When I found out that one man was responsible for both the murders of my brother and my sister, I plotted and I planned. And I waited. I learned everything I could about Michael Carter.

"Then when the opportunity presented itself, I took action against not just Michael Carter, the others who acted in concert with him. Most of his associates were minor players in the drug trade. I sent them all to federal prison for lengthy periods of time. Then I honed in on Sean Branch. I had nothing on him, so I manufactured a case. I stole one kilogram of pure cocaine from the evidence on one of my big cases. Nobody would miss one key. I gave that key of cocaine to Maurice Payne to implicate Sean Branch in a murder he didn't commit. Once that was done, I focused on Michael Carter. Fortuitous enough, Maryann Settles came along and lived on the scene of the Dontay Samuels murder. I paid her to say that Michael Carter killed Samuels. So, there you have it, Ari. I'm guilty as sin. And now this turn of events has changed the timetable—"

"Timetable? What timetable?"

"There's one person out there that I have to send to prison. He's never been to prison. He's gotten away scot free all these years. Until now. Before I leave this office, I have to see this man in cuffs. On his way to prison for decades."

"Who is this man, Greg?" Ari asked inquisitively.

"The child killer who killed my sister. The one that Michael Carter sent. Quran Bashir."

* * *

"Ian, I need you to set up a meeting with Daychelle Spencer—"

"Greg," Ian McNeely looked wounded, "I can't … my career is all—"

"A couple of days ago, you brought Daychelle to me. To listen to her story. Because you knew that she had information about Quran Bashir. The only thing that has changed since that day is the murders of the Settles. I'm innocent of any complicity to that. But my work goes on. If you're not comfortable with the tactics I use with Daychelle, that's fine. You can stay away from what I'm planning. As a matter of fact, I'd prefer it that way. Just give me Daychelle's contact info and I can do the rest."

Ian McNeely wordlessly wrote down all the contact info he had for Daychelle Spencer, then he bolted from my office.

CHAPTER 15

DAVID BATTLE

THE NEXT DAY...
Central Treatment Facility (CTF)
1901 E Street SE

"Niggas in here talking about you out there fuckin' with that broke ass nigga Bow Wow from Woodland. You anything like shit, Tiera."

"You gotta stop listening to niggas in jail, bae. They lie on their dicks and their men dicks."

"So, the dude lying on his dick, huh? Well, how does Bow Wow know where your son goes to school?"

"That boy don't know shit about me—"

"You ain't gotta lie, Tee. His men in here. I showed one of 'em a picture of you and he told me that you fuck with Bow Wow. The nigga Bow Wow told us his man that your house dirty and that your pussy be boofing—"

"Fuck his dirty ass. Broke ass. That nigga asked me for gas money one day when I got him to take me to pick up Trayon. That's how he knew where my son goes to school. All that other shit he talk—"

Upset, I hung up the wall phone on Tiera. She was lying to me and we both knew it. I knew the dude wasn't lying because of two important details. Tiera's house was dirty and her pussy did stink at times. I looked around the unit until I found Jihad standing at the microwave. I walked up and embraced him. "What's up, Slim?"

"I'm cooling, bruh. Thinking about my case and that wild ass nigga Greg Gamble. That nigga tryna bake our asses. The shit he pulling is unheard of. Bugging our cells, though? When the last time you heard about something like that?"

I nodded. "You right. I ain't heard about no shit like that since the Maryland police did that to the Capers homie Fat Rat. You hip to him Slim?"

"Donnell Hunter? Of course I am. Fat Rat shit is legendary in Southeast."

"That's the last time I heard about the people planting a bug in a nigga's cell. It is what it is, though. Fuck Greg Gamble's dick eating ass. What's up with your case. What is your lawyer talking about?"

Jihad broke two Ramen noodles up and added the shrimp flavor packs to them in a bowl. Then he dumped the bowls contents into a popcorn bag. The microwave popcorn bag was best used when frying soups. Jihad opened the microwave and put the bag in it, then set the timer for three minutes. "Same ole shit. I haven't been indicted yet on any murders. Bo's or Denico Autrey's. They don't have no witnesses or a murder weapon. All they got is that grainy video footage of the shootout. Charles Daum said that we gon' spank this shit. I ain't worried about the case. I'm just worried about what them people tryna do with whatever they got from them bugs they planted."

"Same here, Slim, but Zin assured us that the government can't use nothing from the audio they got. The bugs they planted were illegal." I pointed out.

"I'm hip, but I can't lie and say that that shit ain't got me stressed out. I haven't talked to Big Bruh—"

"Me neither and that ain't like him. He ain't answering the 240 number at all. He must've trashed that joint."

"Probably. Especially knowing him like I do, he super 'noid. And Zin ain't say too much about his mind state."

"Because he probably ain't showing his true feelings to her. Quran shit is like a chameleon, Slim. He the best at—"

"BATTLE? CELL 17— DAVID BATTLE!" the unit CO called out.

"Let me go and see what the fuck this pig want, Slim. I probably got a visit or a pass to go somewhere. I'll be right back." I walked up to the male CO that was calling my name. "What's up, CO? I'm cell 17, Battle."

"Bag and baggage, Battle. Just got the call. You're moving back to D.C. jail." the CO said.

My heart sank. There was no way I'd be able to bust the moves I busted at CTF while at D.C. jail.

"That's all. I'm sure they'll let you know where you're going when you go across the cat walk. Hurry up and pack up. Your escort is on the way."

"Fuck!" I muttered as I walked back over to Jihad. "They sending me back over to the jail, Slim. I guess they feel like I healed up enough."

* * *

Forty minutes later…
Central Detention Facility (D.C. Jail)
1901 D Street S.E.

"The adjustment board never saw you about the infraction you caught. Maybe that's because you caught the street charge, I don't know." Lieutenant Ronald Worthy told me. "And you never got to see the housing board to see if you stayed on lockdown. So, congratulations, Champ, you're going to population."

I had to trade in my two piece navy blue CTF uniform for the two piece D.C. jail orange uniform. I fastened the Velcro strap on my white Rawling Tennis shoes and stood up completely. Putting my bag of property in one hand, I put my bedroll under my right arm. "What block I'm going to, Worthy?"

Lt. Worthy looked at the paper in his hand. "You going around the corner, Battle. Southeast three. The MAX block. Let's roll."

* * *

As soon as I walked into Southeast Three's sallyport, I could feel that something was a little off, but I dismissed it as frayed nerves. Any time anybody entered a new housing unit at the jail, inmates crowded around the entrance to see who was coming into the block. This day, it was no different. I said a silent curse word as I thought about the street knife I had with me and hadn't had a chance to put it on me. With a stern look on my face, I surveyed the faces that were visible on the other side of the unit doors.

On the surface, I didn't spot not one enemy face. I was more concerned about the faces that I couldn't see, didn't see.

The female CO was butt ugly and manly. She held the face card that LT. Worthy had given her. "Battle, you're in 73 cell on the bottom right. All the way at the end of the tier. She turned to the man inside the bubble. "Sarge, open two gate."

"What about a mattress?" I asked the C.O.

"I gotta find you one. Gimme a few minutes."

The gate opened and I entered the unit. I quickly walked down the stairs leading to the bottom tier. I needed to get to get to 73 and fish my knife out of my property. I could feel the eyes that followed me. Sense them. I made it to the cell without incident. I could see that the bottom bunk was neatly made and the cell smelled clean. The toilet and sink were immaculate. Dropping the bed roll and bag, I quickly dug out the flip out knife that I'd bought at CTF.

Once the knife's blade was open, I put the weapon on my waist and covered it with the t-shirt I wore under the uniform shirt. Suddenly, I felt secure. My anxiety lessened and I allowed myself to relax. On the desk was an empty cubbyhole. I filled it with my possessions and tossed the bedroll onto the top bunks metal. Someone appeared at the cell door.

I turned to face him, clutching my knife. "What's up? You my celly?"

"Naw, Slim," the big, bald head dude replied. "My name is Big Skye. I'm from First and O Street. I run the block. I'm just pulling up on you to see who you are. What's your name, Slim?"

"Dave." I replied. "I'm from Sheridan Terrace. Southeast."

* * *

"Battle, come and get your mattress." The CO shouted.

Big Skye walked out of my cell. "Go get your mattress, Slim. I'ma holla back at you." I left the cell behind Big Skye. I walked up the steps and grabbed the mattress out of the sally port. Then I carried it down the stairs. Movement behind me caught my attention. When I turned to see the dud coming my way from the shower area, another person appeared in my peripheral. As I dropped the mattress to get my knife out, both men attacked simultaneously. I tried to move quickly, but the two attackers were quicker.

"It's my turn, bitch!" one of the men hissed as he hit me.

I tried to fend off my attackers but they were too much. I looked into the man's face in front of me. The one who'd spoken. Gone were his long dreads, but his face was unmistakable. I was being hit from front and back as I crumpled. I could hear the CO's shouting into walkie talkies as I was being stabbed mercilessly. My last image in my head before the lights went out was the look of venom on Warren Stevenson's face.

CHAPTER 16

SEAN BRANCH

"The investigation into the deaths of a Brandywine, Maryland couple found shot to death in their home four nights ago intensifies. Authorities in Prince Geoge's County are searching for the person or persons involved in the killing of the woman who brought to light Malfeasance and corruption in the United States Attorney's Office. Maryann Settles came forward eighteen years later to recant her trial testimony in the case of Michael Carter.

"In 1996, Mr. Carter was tried and convicted of first degree murder for the killing of sixteen year old Dontay Samuels. At the trial in D.C. Superior Court, Maryann Settles testified that Carter killed Dontay Samuels. After recanting her 1996 trial testimony, Maryann Settles appeared recently in post post-conviction hearing to have Michael Carter's conviction overturned. At that hearing, Mrs. Settles cited her religious beliefs and desire to right her past wrongs as the reason to come forward and reveal that she was paid by then AUSA Gregory Gamble to lie and give perjured testimony about Carter. AUSA Susan Rosenthal was also implicated in the wrong doing…

"In other news today, D.C. Police are investigating the overnight killing of a Northeast man now identified as 54 year old Andre Clea. The Central Detention Facility has been placed on an indefinite lockdown. D.C. jail while law enforcement investigates the death of one of its inmates in his housing unit. Sources close to Fox news have told us that errors were made that cost David Battle his life. Our sources revealed that a couple months ago, David Battle stabbed a man identified as Warren Stevenson in a different housing unit inside the jail. Weeks later, while leaving an attorney visit Javon Jarrett attacked Mr. Battle and stabbed him several times. A stabbing that we were told was retaliation for the stabbing of Warren Stevenson.

"David Battle was moved across the street to CTF medical unit while he recovered from his injuries. Here's where errors were made, we were told. After there has been serious assaults perpetrated on inmates, both inmates or all inmates involved in the assault have to be separated… a process called a 'Keep Separate' from one another. In this case, that didn't happen. While housed at CTF, Warren Stevenson came from a local hospital back to D.C. jail. There was no 'Keep Separate' order lodged for Stevenson and Battle. David Battle was moved from CTF's medical unit back to the jail. He was mistakenly placed in the same housing unit with the man he was charged with stabbing months ago.

"Warren Stevenson and Chomondre Paige have been moved out of the D.C. jail. How ironic was that? All the people that Quran had killed to get him home and look at what happened. The audio from Jihad's cell that was bugged. All the shit that Jihad had told Dave. About the murders of his witnesses. The murders of his homie Mann, the uncle of the woman he killed. That brought on thoughts of the murder. The murder of Quran's younger brother Khitab. A murder that Quran committed after learning that Khitab was one of the witnesses against Dave Battle."

"Damn." I uttered to myself. "All for nothing."

I could hear Dave Battle's voice in my head as he talked and laughed and joked with Jihad in the cell. Then there was silence. Empty noise. Noise that represented the fact that

David Battle was gone. From this life at least. I thought about something else the news broadcast had said. All the stuff about Greg Gamble, Mike Carter and Maryann Settles. Somebody had finally gotten to the female rat. Killed her and her husband. I smiled at that. Because even though she came back and recanted years later, the fact doesn't change that she ratted.

I laughed to myself thinking about all the people who'd say that Maryann Settles was a civilian, thereby justifying her snitching. Some people would say that her being a woman is different. Shaking my head, I disagreed with all that shit. Maryann Settles was in the streets, hustling, drugging, getting arrested. The code of Omerta applied to her, too. She told on Mike Carter to avoid going to prison. Paid or not paid to snitch. That made her a vicious RAT. I sat in the storage unit on the floor and wondered who had finally gotten to her. Was it Quran? Killing her for Mike Carter? Or was it Mike Carter? Ordering her death from his cell despite the fact that the woman resurfaced to recant her trial testimony and free him after almost nineteen years.

Knowing Mike Carter like I did, it was probably him. Nobody could hold a grudge like Mike Carter. And me. The more I thought about Mike Carter, the more my soul ached to kill him. If Quran hesitated even a little bit, I vowed to kill him. Painfully. No bullets to the head. That would be too easy a way to die. I needed Mike Carter to suffer before he died. Suffer real bad.

Movement to my left made me look in that direction. I saw a woman helping an older woman into a wheelchair, then wheel the chair to a handicap accessible van that waited by the curb in front of the house on 63rd Street in Northeast. I stared openly through the window at the woman in the wheel chair. The resemblance to her son was uncanny. Quickly, I exited the Tundra and crossed the street. Both women eyed me as I approached.

"Can I help you?" I asked the woman whose uniform's logo matched the one emblazoned across the van. McGruder's Access Transit.

"I think I can manage, sir," the woman responded.

"And you must be Wilhemena Shaw? Rodney's mom."

The old woman smiled as she looked at me. "That's right. And who are you, baby?"

"You can call me death." I pulled my gun and killed both women.

CHAPTER 17

TOMASINA

The inside of my apartment was cold as shit. And just the way I liked it. I hate heat. Especially while I was sleeping. For some reason, I tended to sleep better in the winter. That's why a window in my bedroom stayed cracked open. To let the air in. Although I hated heat, I loved warmth and warmth was what I was, luxuriating under the thick comforter on my King size bed. The incessant vibrating of my cellphone was threatening to drive me crazy. It had already broken my sleep and had me irritated. I continued to ignore the phone and tried to go back to the place where good sleep lived, but it wasn't meant to be. The cellphone was winning the round. I reached my arm from under the comforter and grabbed the phone from off the table next to the bed. I answered the phone without even looking at it.

"Hello? What the fuck…What?"

"Bitch, are you woke?" Tushonda asked.

"I am now. Your pressed ass made sure of that." I replied.

"I been calling your ass since yesterday. Where are you?"

"I am at home. In bed. Where I've been since day before yesterday. All of them double shifts finally caught up with my ass. Not to mention all the good dick I been getting. I was tired as shit. Still am. Fuck is so important that you been ringing my phone like you the IRS?"

"So, you haven't heard? I knew that you didn't know."

109

"Didn't know what?" I said and sat up in bed. "Haven't heard what?"

"About the inmate you used to pull out all the time. The one that got stabbed in the visiting hall at D.C. jail."

At the mention of D.C. jail, my phone pinged rapidly to alert me to all the missed calls I had. "Stabbed over at the jail? Who, David Battle?"

"Yeah, him. Bitch, he got moved back to D.C. jail yesterday and somebody killed him—"

"What? Wait... no, you can't be serious. I just left him—"

"Tam, the shit been all over the news. The Director shut the jail down. It's on indefinite lockdown. David Battle was mistakenly put into a unit with the dude he stabbed months ago. That dude and another dude killed him as soon as he got in the unit early yesterday—"

I knew that Tushonda was still talking. I could hear her, but I wasn't listening. My mind was elsewhere. All I could think about was one thing. Quran Bashir and the havoc he was about to wreak on the world. I hung up the phone on Tushonda and immediately dialed Quran's number.

"Come on, Quran, pick up the phone." I begged.

* * *

The game that I was playing was a dangerous one, but I was dedicated to playing it. For as much as I wanted Quran Bashir dead, bringing about his demise was to be done my way. So, I had to play my part. The part that I had been playing for years. Quran Bashir walked onto a porch in May of 1995 and he killed my oldest brother. Shot him down like a dog and left him to die of his wounds. That irrefutable fact angered me as it saddened me for most of my life.

I moved around as a teen in all different circles of women and yet the stories about the incredibly handsome grey eyed man were all the same. Quran Bashir was beautiful on the eyes. He was a complete thug with off the charts swag. He was super fly, sexy and as deadly as the Ebola virus. Rumored to be killing since his childhood, Quran's gun game was legendary. As I became overly sexually active, I searched for the right man that I could eventually send to kill Quran. A man that I could seduce physically, emotionally and mentally. Someone that my pussy, ass or mouth or the combination of all three could control. All I found were cowards, down low niggas and fake mother fuckers. Not one person that I could use to kill Quran.

Then I thought that maybe I could kill him myself. Just trick him somewhere and blow his fucking brains out. But quickly I learned that I wasn't someone who could violently kill another person. I wasn't like him. Like Quran. I wasn't like my brother Dontay, who I'd heard had killed several men. I wasn't built like them. Years passed and I had almost given up my desire to see my brother's murder avenged, but then I learned two things that changed my life. The first thing I learned was that I had contracted HIV. That revelation in itself almost broke me, but I persevered. Although, I was emotionally bankrupt and in a dark place, I couldn't forget about the vow I had made to my brother when I was kid. The vow to avenge his death.

Another thing I learned was that time waits for no one, so I bided mine. Bided, plotted, planned and executed. I got closer to Tosheka until meeting Quran was inevitable. After meeting him and getting closer to know him, I still planned. Then one night while at Tosheka's house, I struck. Pretending to be pissy drunk, I came on to Quran while Tosheka was passed out. And just like any man would, Quran took the bait. That first time, I sucked his dick. Well. Overtime, whenever opportunity presented itself, I ate his dick over and over again. Swallowing his seed each time. I knew that it would only be a matter of time before Quran and I took the next step and had sex. Then once sex began, the time would come. The time for me to introduce Quran Bashir to the wonderful world of AIDS.

* * *

"Go ahead and lean your seat back." I told Riley Patterson.

"Right here?" he replied.

"Yeah, right here. Right now. In this car. Move your seat back some and then lean it back so my head will be away from the steering wheel."

Riley did exactly as I instructed. I pulled off my Ugg boots one at a time and then unloosened my belt on my jeans. I removed my coat and threw it into the back of the Range Rover. My sweater came off next. I wanted to be as comfortable as I possibly could as I worked my mojo on the man who worked in the records office at the D.C. jail. Although, Quran hadn't answered my call all day, I knew exactly what he wanted, exactly what he needed. And I knew exactly how to get it for him.

I climbed over onto Riley's side of the truck and positioned myself on my knees in front of him. With his eyes entranced and staring right at me, I unzipped Riley's pants and pulled out his dick. For what he lacked in length, his dick made up for it in girth. I stroked the thick dick in my hand a few times until the precum appeared. After licking my glossed lips, I put his dick in my mouth and snatched his soul.

* * *

Thirty minutes later...

"What exactly do you need, Tomasina?" Riley asked me.

"I need for you to pull the files of the two inmates charged in the murder of the other inmate yesterday. Warren Stevenson and Shamondre Paige. Pull their files and use your phone to screenshot everything you see in the files. Then you can text all you find to me on my phone. Can you handle that?"

"Of course, I can, but what do you need all that for? What's your interest in them?"

"The less you know the better, Riley."

"I can end up inside a cell at the jail for what you're asking me to do, Tomasina. At least tell me what you plan to do with what I find."

"Do you think my pussy good, Riley?" I asked all of a sudden.

"I think it is. You are a sexy mothafucka."

"I tell you what, baby. Let's find out. Has that dick recovered from what my mouth did to it, yet?"

Riley smiled, unzipped his fly and pulled out his hardening dick. "I think so."

"Stroke that fat dick for me, Riley."

Riley did what I told him to do.

"Would you like to see if my pussy good, Riley?"

"Fuck yeah. I wanna se—"

"As thick as you are, you might hurt me, but I'm a thorough bitch. You wanna feel how tight this pussy is? And see how wet it get?"

"Can I? Can I please, Toma—"

I watched Riley stroke his dick in anticipation of getting some pussy. "As soon as you get me what I asked you for, you can get this pussy. Agreed?"

"C'mon, Tomasina… with that shit. You got me all rock hard, I'm tryna fuck right now." Riley pleaded.

I leaned over and kissed Riley's cheek, then went down and kissed his dick. "Get me the contents of them files. Then you can have this pussy all you want."

With that said, I zipped up my coat and hopped out of the Range Rover.

* * *

As the Vietnamese lady in Beautiful Nails gave my feet a massage after extracting them from the hot water tub at the bottom of the salon chair. I patiently waited for the text message that would hit my phone soon.

"What color polish for your toes?" Tammy, the Vietnamese lady, asked.

"You decide, Tammy. Just make sure it's pretty."

* * *

Standing in front of the full length mirror attached to the closet door in my bedroom, I looked at myself. In that mirror, I saw the girl I used to be and the woman I had become. I looked for signs of attrition and found none. My caramel complexion was radiant and continued to glow like always. My brown eyes sparkled. At five foot four inches barefoot, everything about me was proportioned just right. My breasts were firm and perky. My ass was phat and jiggled when smacked. My hands and feet were always complimented. In other words, I was flawless. By looking at me, no one could tell that I was a beautiful, walking nuclear reactor.

Thoughts of my status made me think about a conversation I had recently with my good friend Jackie.

"... You better slow your ass down before you end up honeymooning in Vegas out here... that new dick be coming with issues. Baby mamas, side bitched, drama and that honeymoon in Vegas."

"Tam, chill out with all that shit. Don't you know that words got power? Don't speak no shit like that into the universe."

"I feel you but let me ask you this before I go. What would your crazy ass do if you did catch that shit?"

"Fuck you think I'ma do? Give that shit right back to other niggas. Shit —I wouldn't be the only motherfuckin' dummy out here sick. Niggas would get this pussy gift wrapped and handed to 'em. It's the gift that keeps on giving."

Every joke has a degree of truth in it. I often joked with my friends about HIV but none of them knew that I had it. Only certain family members knew my secret. People that I wanted to know. I rubbed my titties through the halter top I had on. Then I put my fingers between my legs to see if my panties were wet in the middle. They were. I could have any man I wanted whenever I wanted, but I was single by choice. Singling while mingling is what I described my lifestyle as. I was doing exactly what Jackie had said she'd do. Give away the gift that keeps on giving.

The only difference with me was that I didn't give my gift to everyone; only the unfortunate ones that found ways to stoke my ire. There'd been a few guys from the past that I tried to give my gift, but I don't know if I succeeded or not. That's why Quran would be different, had been different. The chance of passing the virus to another person via oral sex was slim to none. But in Quran's case, I'd been giving him sloppy, saliva-drenched head for at least three years in spots. Recently things had progressed. I'd given him the pussy several times in the last month, but only one time was our sex unprotected.

Then I remembered the day Quran fucked my ass for close to an hour it seemed. He'd been in my ass raw. Maybe I gave him the gift that day. Maybe it was the other day, when we got busy in my car. I remembered riding Quran's big dick raw dog. I wondered if the gift was passed then. Hopefully, it was, but if it wasn't, I still had plenty of time to gift it to him. I just had to be smart, be patient and pick my shots wisely. I know that Quran had a new bitch that he loved, but I gave zero fucks about her. This had nothing… well, eventually it would, but right now this had nothing to do with her. Everything to do with him.

Those fleeting thoughts of me riding Quran's dick made me horny. My pussy was already wet; all it needed was proper stimulation to make me orgasm. After that, I'd smoke me a jay of weed and wait to hear from Riley.

* * *

The text messages came through from Riley at 8:19 pm. I text him back and set up a time and place for us to rendezvous on my next day off. After that I sent a text to Quran.

//: Call me when you can, I have something that you need. And my condolences to you and David's family. May he rest in peace.

I was thinking about David Battle and whether or not I'd given him the gift, when my cellphone vibrated. Excited, I grabbed the phone, thinking that the caller was Quran. It wasn't. The caller was Bionca.

"Hey, Bionca, baby, what's good?" I sang into the phone with veiled fakeness.

"Hey, Tom. How are you? Were you busy or at work?"

"Naw, I'm good. At home on my day off. Chilling. Alone."

"I'm sorry to hear that, but listen, I got a question for you and I'm hoping that you can help me out."

"I will if I can, gurl. Shoot."

"You were equally as close to Tosheka as I was. That fine ass nigga that she was in love with, the one with the grey eyes—"

"Quran. His name is Quran, but go ahead, my bad."

"Yeah, him. Would you happen to know how I can get in touch with him?"

"Who Quran? You tryna get in touch with Quran?"

"Yeah," Bionca answered.

"Can I ask why?" I asked.

"You can ask, but no need to because I'll tell you. I'm tryna get at his friend Sean Branch\ and—"

"Sean Branch? The old head Sean Branch?"

"Yeah. I need to get with him about some shit and I don't know nobody who might know how I can find him. Then I

116

remembered that Tosh told me that Quran and Sean Branch were friends. Can you help me?"

"B, I'm just a regular ole CO bitch making coins off the District government and that takes up most of my time with how much they work me. I'm six degrees separated form the streets. So, the answer is no. I don't know nobody who's in contact with that fine ass, grey eyed nigga Quran. And I definitely don't know nobody that runs with the old head Sean Branch. I ain't tryna go around nobody that be with him. My nosey ass coworkers at work talking about he out here cutting off heads and shit. Carrying them around with him. If I find out something that can help you, Bionca, I promise to call you. Okay?"

"Aight, Tom. You do that. Thanks, girl. Take care."

"I will and you do the same. Bye"

Disconnecting the call, I tossed the cellphone onto the couch next to me. Sneaky bitch. Everybody in the city knows by now that Sean Branch is rumored to have killed both of her brothers. Word was that he was the person who cut off her brother Crud's head off and left with it. That was the reason why I mentioned that aspect of Sean Branch's reputation, to let her know I knew. The question in my head was, did Bionca really want access to Quran JUST to possibly get to Sean Branch or did she want to harm Quran as well?

I wasn't sure of what Bionca Clark's true motive for wanting to get in contact with Quran was, but if her motive was his alleged participation in her brother's death and she wanted him dead. She'd have to get in line. Quran Bashir's demise was mine to claim.

CHAPTER 18

BIONCA CLARK

"Sis, this shit is just like D.C." Brechelle said. "Baby Southeast. I thought that moving down here would get me away from guns and violence, but I was wrong. These niggas down here is on that gang shit hard as hell. Blooding and Cripping like they out California somewhere. They got one fuckin' mall in Winston Salem, Be. One. And you can't really go there without some shit jumping off. These white people down here sick and tired of these niggas, girl. They all but saying it every time you turn on the local news. Auntie Brenda 'nem live in the neighborhood called Piedmont Circle. Auntie Bernadine and Grandma Birdie live on 25th Street. I'm staying in Rolling Hills with Toya, Crissy and Zandy and all these neighborhoods beef with each other. I might get shot visiting our relatives."

"Well, don't get shot, Bre. Or better yet, don't go visit the relatives." I told my younger sister. "Hopefully, soon, you'll be able to come home. I just don't want you here until—"

"Say less, sis. I'm good, though. Really, I am. It's okay down here, for real, for real. Other than the goofy shit. I'm close to Mama. I go to her gravesite every other day and talk to her. I put fresh flowers on her tombstone—"

"Is it cold out there, Bre?"

"A little, but not as frigid as it is up there. This is the South, you know."

"I know. Well, look, let me go and finish my work. Give my love to the family and you be safe down there. Call me if you need anything. Anything Be, again, I'm sorry to hear about Celine. I know how you felt about her."

"Thanks, Bre, but really I'm good. Considering the circumstances. I'm determined to make sure that we don't lose anyone else. Feel me."

"I feel you. Have you decided what to do with Mama's house?"

"That is your house, Bre. Our house. Whatever is decided, it'll be decided by you and me. Don't worry about nothing. We gon' be good. Just chill out down there and stay out of the way of them wild ass niggas down there. Okay?"

"Okay. I love you, Bionca. You be safe up there, too. Bye."

I wiped away tears as I ended the call with my sister. Then I laid the cellphone down on the dining room table. I took a moment to compose myself before talking to Ren or her mother who were both eating Wing Stop chicken wings and fries. "Getting rid of your Infiniti Truck, Ren was a smart move. I need to get rid of my car, too. Even though the title, registration and insurance is in my name, everything has the Southern Avenue address on it. Sean already knows I live there. He's been there. He has no other way to find me, other than that address."

"The Infiniti was in my name and the address I used was the Ivy City address, not this one. Same goes for my driver's license. I wasn't working and the lease to this place is in somebody's name Brion knew. He got somebody to do that CPN shit. I just pay the rent… well, he paid it before, but I pay it now. I got rid of the Infiniti because I drove it to all the places where Brion and I left bodies at. What about you, Ma?"

Dorenda Tyler looked up from her chicken before licking her fingers to remove the Ranch dressing and sauces that congealed there. "I am a licensed RN, so anybody can probably find that online. That and the fact that I work at George Washington University Hospital. But other than that, my address was my ruined house on Decatur Street. Sean knows that. Just like Bionca's house, he's been there. My car, banking information, everything, has that address. All my identification, everything. I don't have no social media accounts or none of that tip drawing ass shit. Sean can probably find out that I drive a grey Chrysler 300, but there's thousands of 'em on these streets in D.C. and Maryland. I love my car. I'm not getting rid of it, because of Sean Branch or ISIS. Next subject."

"Well, honestly, I don't know what else we could do." I confessed, exasperated. "We been on computers for days and combing the streets and still nothing. NOTHING!"

Ren used her fork to move food around her Styrofoam container. "There has to be something else we can do to find him. At the moment, I just don't know what that is."

"I tried everything I could think of. Nobody in the streets has seen Sean. If they have, no one is gonna tell us they have. He's not hanging out anywhere. He's not on Saratoga Avenue, Montana Avenue or in Brentwood anywhere. He's rumored to be killing all of his past enemies everywhere. He's from Langdon Park. He damn near wiped out an entire family because… according to the streets… he thought some dude named Moe Best's family killed his daughter. He's not on R Street on either the Northeast or Northwest side. Nobody knows where he could be. And to make matters worse, he doesn't have any vices that people know of. No vulnerable spots. No family members left that we can pinpoint and he's a lone wolf. We can't even find the one dude that's linked to him. Quran Bashir. He's suddenly invisible on the streets. All we can do is keep doing what we've been doing and pray that Sean Branch surfaces soon. End of story."

CHAPTER 19

ZIN

"At the end of the day, Zin, I think you're being too hard on your father."

Shaking my head, I rolled the chocolate chip cookie dough under my hands. "I should've known that you'd take his side. It never fails."

"Hey," Linda Carter protested as she turned around from the stove. "That's not fair to me. I try to never take sides between you and your dad. I'm like a NFL referee, I'm neutral. I love both of you guys equally. I'm just saying how I feel from what I see—"

"Well, guess what, auntie. My mother *can't see*. Because she's dead! Killed by your brother."

"You don't know that as fact! So, stop what you're doing, Zin. With that attitude, you can only make things worse. That letter from your Mom doesn't...can't possibly say who caused her death. You are essentially taking the word of who? Delores Samuel's? Ameen Bashir's son? Quran? The first person hates Mike because her son was killed. And the second who now thinks Mike killed his father. Neither of them make for good sources of truthful insight."

"And my father is the epitome of truthful insight, right?"

"Look, this is not an academic debate between aunt and niece. I'm just say—"

"Auntie, I hear everything you're saying, but you're not hearing me. All I asked that man was for some honesty. If he couldn't muster honesty, he could've just gave me realism. He couldn't even do that. I would have respected him more if he would have gave me lies mixed in with a little truth. Had he just accepted whatever he wanted to accept, but still explained what happened to my mom, I could've accepted that. Win, lose or draw. We could've bumped heads about the details and gotten mad or even cursed each other out. I could respect any of that. But your brother did none of it. He cowardly just walked away. Turned and left. Without a word. Who does that? What kinda father does that to his daughter? A daughter just seeking answers to good questions. Huh? Answer that, auntie? Can you?"

The lamb chops were starting to burn. My aunt turned to pay attention to them. "I'm not gonna make any excuses for Mike. I can't. I don't even want to. In my life experience, I've just learned to be more objective and I see things differently than a person who's your age. For as bad as things may seem, I don't want you to be opposed to whatever olive branch your father extends. When he extends it. Because no matter what, he's—"

"Still your father." I said finishing my aunt's sentence. "And how many times have I heard you say that?"

My aunt Linda turned around again. "However many times I need to say it. We're family, Zin. Me, you and him. No ill feelings you might have is gonna change that. So what, you're beefing with him today. And even tomorrow. Just remember that there's always room for reconciliation. Always."

Suddenly, I stopped rolling cookie dough. "I let you talk, Auntie and I heard you out. Really, I did. And you are perceptive, charismatic and smart. I often agree with you on a lot of issues. But I don't think I'ma be able to do it on this one." I got up from the table and left the kitchen.

"ZIN! ZIN! Come back here! ZIN!"

* * *

I walked through my door prepared to deal with Quran and his grief about his friend David, but to my surprise, the condo was empty. Quran was nowhere to be found. I shook my coat off and sat on the couch to pull my boots off. Stripping down to just panties and the blouse I was wearing, I made myself a cup of hot chocolate. I could feel the fetus inside me moving. I was three months pregnant and showing. Standing in the kitchen, I rubbed my belly and thought about Quran. There had been shelter for his pain. He couldn't hide it.

I remembered the exact time he'd gotten a call from someone. I never learned who the caller had been. I just remember seeing the man that I love crumble. He sat on the couch in my living room and fell apart. He screamed, he cried, he punched the air, he paced, he mumbled, he talked to himself aloud. In the time we'd been a couple, he'd experienced nothing but death around him. Yet, I couldn't remember a time that he reacted so distraught. Inconsolable. Broken. The day that Quran had killed his brother Khitab, I hadn't seen the level of emotion that I witnessed when he found out that David had been killed after being sent back to D.C. jail.

Pulling the hot drink from the microwave, I sipped it. The chocolaty goodness burned my tongue, but I ignored that. My mind was on David Battle. I thought about all the times I'd gone to see him. All the conversations we'd had, good and bad. I thought about the way his eyes lit up when he talked about Quran. I thought the sinister thoughts I'd had several times over the last four months thinking that Khitab's warnings to Quran that 'Dave is going to cross you' would come true. And when I thought about all the times I had asked Quran, 'Do you trust David?' And every time, Quran's answer had been the same. "I trust him with my life."

Tears welled in my eyes and fell. I thought about Javon Jarrett stabbing David in the visiting room. I remembered feeling sick thinking that David might die as I left the jail that day. I thought about the day David decided to leave Wentz and Locks and became my first client once I started my own practice. I thought about the fact that David shouldn't even had still been in jail. Had he never stabbed Warren Stevenson... he wouldn't be dead.

Going back to the living room, I found my phone in my purse. I had several missed calls, most from my Aunt Linda and none from Quran. I dialed Quran's cellphone, waited, but got no answer.

"Quran, where are you?"

CHAPTER 20

QURAN

1351 Havard Road
Southeast, D.C.

"I'm on my lunchbreak, Quran, and I only get an hour." Tomasina announced as soon as she was inside the apartment. "Smells like big weed in here. Where's it at?"

I crossed the living room and pulled out the Ziplock bag of Sante Rondo Valley OG. I passed the bag to Tomasina.

Tomasina handed it back. "I don't need the whole pack. Roll one up while I talk." Tom removed her coat and Nike boots. Then sat across from me on the couch. I rolled up the weed. "I know you got my text. As soon as I heard about David, I jumped into action. The shit I do for your fine ass. I remembered that you wanted to know about the dude who stabbed David at the jail. So, I knew you'd want information on the two niggas who killed him. God bless the dead and all that. I got in touch with a friend—"

"The classification nigga from last time?" I asked as I sealed the blunt.

"Naw. Couldn't go back to that well to get wet. Nigga would've asked too many questions and I didn't want that. I used another nigga that's been begging me to fuck—"

I lit the blunt, puffed it twice, inhaled then walked it to Tomasina. "Did you fuck him?"

"Fuck no. I did what I always do. Make a rack of empty promises." Tomasina said and puffed on the blunt several times. She coughed violently which brought tears to her eyes and a smile to mine. "Damn! Fuck this come from the weed Gods?" After coughing a little more, Tomasina calmed down. "I'm a vicious dick tease, Que. Anyway, he…my friend in records at the jail… sent me this." Tomasina grabbed her phone and pulled up the screen shots that she'd gotten from the dude.

Her phone was one of the newer iPhone, so her screen was larger than most phone screens. I used two fingers to enlarge the parts of the page that I need to see. I grabbed my phone and took pictures of Tomasina's phone screen. By the time I looked up from the phone, the blunt was gone and Tomasina's pants were off. Smiling, I said, "Stop what you are doing, Tom. I ain't in the mood for no fucking."

"Who said anything about us fucking, Que?" Tomasina replied as her fingers moved around inside her panties. She leaned all the way back and made a show out of fingering herself. "I didn't… plan on doing this…aww-w shit… I just… wanted… to… to… shit… get you… this info… on them… on them… two… dudes! It's the… it's… the… weed… that… got me… horny… as shit!"

I couldn't help but laugh at Tomasina. "You crazy as shit, Tom. And I needed a good laugh."

"Glad… I… I… could… help. Now… put… your… dick...in… my mouth!"

The addresses and contact info for both Warren Stevenson and Chamondre Paige was exactly what I needed to see. The level of love and respect I had for Tomasina gave me no choice but to comply with her wishes. I dropped the phones and walked over to Tom. I pulled my dick free and gave it to her. "Here. Enjoy."

* * *

"Quran…please…stop! Please, stop! Ugh… oww…oooh… stop!"

"Shut up and take this dick!" I hissed into Tomasina's face as I held her feet on my shoulders and pounded her pussy deep.

"Stop… S…S…S…t…t…t…o…o…p! Pl…e.e.a.s.s.e!"

"Stop what? Stop what, Tom?"

"Stop… fuckin'… me… like … this! Ugh…ugh… owww! Put… put … my feet down! Put… my… feet… down… QURAN!"

"Am I fuckin' you good?"

"Y-y-y-e-e-s-s-s!"

"You started this, Tom! You did this!"

"I gotta go back to work, Quran! Please… Stop!"

"Can I cum in this pussy?"

"Yes…please! Please cum in me!"

"Damn, this pussy good! Pussy good as shit! Ugghh…!"

I kissed Tomasina's forehead and came deep in her pussy. I was exhausted.

* * *

Standing under the hot spray of shower water, I leaned my forehead onto the shower wall. I thought again about my partner Dave and cried. I couldn't believe the way life was. Karma was real. Allah's wrath was real. Both of those truths made sense but collided with one another. Those truths were contradictions that lived in me. If one truly believed in Allah and that everything was preordained by Allah, then there was no room for belief in Karma. But yet, I believed in them both. Both in total contrast to one another.

I thought about the entire picture that had led to Dave's death. He killed Manny Robinson for robbing his lil man. After being in jail for months, he learned that Yolanda Stevens and his cousin Black Tommy were witnesses against him. He reached out to me and I killed both witnesses. Then

I had to kill Landa's uncle, Mann because he would've killed me had he even heard I killed his niece. Then came the death of my brother Tabu. A murder that had to happen once I learned that he was the last remaining witness against Dave.

My tears came even harder as I remembered the night I killed him. Zin by my side. He had violated the code by agreeing to snitch on Dave. There was no way in the world that I could let that happen. I could have done what Jihad had suggested and sent my brother away from D.C., but I was too offended and hurt by his treachery. After that, Dave's release was all but assured. Then he stabbed the dude Warren Stevenson.

Warren Stevenson's man attacked Dave and stabbed him. For that crime, I found Warren's man, Jaron Jarrett's brother and killed him. But that hadn't been enough. Dave was sent from CTF back to D.C. and inadvertently placed in the same unit with Warren Stevenson. He in turn, ambushed Dave with the help of another dude and killed him. I couldn't believe the events and how they unfolded. I turned off the shower water and got myself together. By the time I dried off and got dressed, I was ready for what came next. Killing.

* * *

543 Taylor Street N.E.

The neighborhood where the house is stood is considered residential. Most, if not all, of the homes had cameras attached to them. I drove around the block a few times before stopping to observe the beige brick two story house on Taylor St. The houses were all connected to one another, but separated by different style gates in front and fences in back of the houses. 543 was the second house from the corner and three blocks from the Fort Totten metro station. According to the file on Warren Stevenson, his mother Trinity and three siblings lived at the house on Taylor St. The file didn't provide ages for the siblings or the mother, but it didn't matter.

I sat in the Genesis and thought about my past motto, no women, no children. But in this case, I'd make an exception. The lights were on inside the house despite the late hour. I filed that memory as I pulled away from the curb and headed to my next destination. The file for Chemondre Paige had two addresses listed. Andre Milton lived on Ely Place off of Minnesota Avenue in Southwest. In a building with the numbers 3600 painted on its facade. He lived in apartment #325 with his girlfriend, Cymbal Gaffney, and their 10 year old son, Ceandre. Chendra Paige lived in Congress Park on 14th Place. Her address was a project tenement that looked rundown. I spotted no cameras on any of the project tenements. I smiled as I drove down Congress Street. The projects were always perfect locations for murders.

* * *

The next morning...

"I think you should go over to CTF and visit Jihad." Zin said.

"I don't really do jails." I replied and turned over in bed. Zin moved around her bedroom as she got dressed for work. "I get that, but I think he needs to see you now. Talk to you. Especially now since what's happened to David."

"I hear you. I'ma figure something out. It has been a while since I talked to him."

"And what if he thinks you got David killed—"

"Jay would never think no stupid ass shit like that. Besides, the exact circumstances behind Dave's murder has been all over the news and in the newspaper. The Washington Post online had an article about the director of the D.C. Department of Corrections getting fired yesterday. The mayor talked about how dangerous the D.C. jail is. Jay watches the news. He knows that I ain't have nothing… wouldn't have nothing to do with no shit like that."

"You're right, you're right. I was just thinking about our last visit when him and David seemed so visibly afraid that them talking about you in their cells, was going to get them both killed. Then days later, David is murdered. I just thought… you know what, never mind. I still think that you should go and see your brother. CTF has contact visits. They can't monitor what y'all talk about like D.C. jail could. That's just my two cents. Think about it."

I laid on my back with my hands folded behind my head and stared at the ceiling. Maybe Zin was right. It was time for me to go and check in on my brother.

CHAPTER 21

GREG GAMBLE

Office of Professional Responsibility
901 Pennsylvania Ave N.W.

The D.C. jail where a man was recently killed has failed to protect incarcerated people from violence and other abuses, federal officials said Thursday. In a 97 page report, the Justice Department described conditions at the D.C. jail as dangerous and unsanitary. Alleging that jail officials use excessive force, the facility is in disrepair and inmates are denied adequate medical and health care. Federal investigators documented violent incidents, including the death of another inmate who was stabbed 20 times in January and the death of another inmate who was strangled by his cellmate in December of last year.

"We cannot continue to turn a blind eye to the inhumane, violent and hazardous conditions people are subject to inside the D.C. jail." Assistant United States Attorney Susan Rosenthal said in a news conference yesterday.

In its report, the Justice Department outlined remedial steps, including reducing contraband at the jail, improving the physical conditions of the facility and ensuring that the inmates receive adequate medical and health services. The D.C. jail has a population of 1,823 inmates, a marked decrease from 2,500 it held three years ago. Within weeks of the launch of the Justice Department's investigation, violence erupted at the jail, with seven people stabbed and one inmate killed during a 24 hour period in August of 2012. Since then six people have been killed at the D.C. jail. Investigators said that last year there were 1,054 assaults, and 314 stabbings. A higher rate than jails in other big cities.

The report also documented assaults by inmates targeting people perceived as gay, lesbian or transgender.

"Greg Gamble?" a voice called out.

"That's me." I replied.

The voice belonged to the white, female secretary. "You can go in now."

I folded the Washington Post newspaper and put it back on the table. Rising from my seat, the woman directed me to a conference room. When I walked into the room, I was surprised to see all the people who I was scheduled to meet with in the coming weeks all assembled together. In the room, seated around the table were Paul Danielson, Brad Shaub, Burt Ryans, Stephen Ross and D.C. Mayor Yvette Bowers. They all stood to greet me.

"Greg, we're all glad that you could make it." Burt Ryans, who heads the Office of Professional Responsibility started. "And I knew that you've met with Brad Shaub recently. So, you already know basically what this meeting is about."

"I do know what it's about."

"Good, so we needn't waste time with all the details. This recent situation where you were accused of malfeasance, corruption and other bad acts, it's not good for the city right now. We all here have talked about this over the last few days and we are a consensus that believe that although you have a due process right, and should be given the opportunity to prove your innocence in these matters, the circus atmosphere and the fallout is what we'd like to avoid—"

"If I may interject," Attorney General Paul Danielson chimed in. "Everyone here appreciates the way you've run the U.S. Attorney's office for the last decade. And on behalf of everyone here, we salute you for your service to the

District of Columbia. We thank you for your tireless effort to reduce crime in the city. But, I have to be completely honest when I say that in light of the murders of Maryann Settles and her husband Christopher, we cannot continue to act like we don't hear or see the implication ramifications attached to you and this investigation. We cannot turn a blind eye to the fact that the whole situation in conjunction with the allegations lodged against you, is not already being judged in the court of public opinion—"

"So, in short," Mayor Bowers said. "You have sixty days to either retire or resign from your position as United States Attorney for the District of Columbia or be fired. You were appointed U.S. Attorney by my predecessor and you've served in that capacity for over a decade. I will not hesitate to relieve you of the office you hold So, gracefully bow out, Greg or be cast out. Your choice."

"You'll have my resignation faxed to each one of you in the next few weeks," I replied, stood up and left the room.

* * *

U.S. Attorney's Office
555 4th St. N.W.

"Daychelle, before you go in the next room and testify in front of that grand jury that's paneled, we need to talk. Everything that you told me last week, you have to repeat to the grand jury. But I need you to do me and yourself a favor. Do you want justice for your friend Kendra?"

Daychelle Spencer nodded.

"How bad do you want justice for KD?"

"Real bad."

"Sometimes the truth is shrouded in lies, Daychelle. Believe that?"

Daychelle nodded.

"Lies can be bad and sometimes lies can be good. Do you understand that?"

IF YOU CROSS ME ONCE 6 | ANTHONY FIELDS

"Yes."

"Okay, listen, Andy Daniels introduced y'all to his cousin. That's what you told me, right?"

"Yes."

"Told you that his name was Quintez or Quintay, correct?"

"No. Andy didn't tell us that, I don't think. Que told us his name was Quintay."

"Okay. Andy's cousin who told you his name was Quintay wanted to buy weed from Kendra, correct?"

"Yes. He asked for twenty pounds."

"Right. So, a meeting was set up for Que to get the weed. Whose idea was it for y'all to meet up at the bus depot at Union Station?"

"That was KD... Kendra's idea. The bus depot was close to the Cordas, it was deserted at certain times, but it was still public enough to keep niggas from trying shit. Excuse my language."

"Excused, but when you get in front of them white folks in there, try to refrain from cursing and using the N word. Getting back to the meet. You told me earlier today that it was common practice for Kendra to want to count the money before she gave up the drugs, correct?"

Daychelle nodded. "She wanted to make sure the money was always real and that the entire amount was counted for no matter how much money it was supposed to be. That's why we always went to meets in two cars. Kendra would never be near the drugs. The weed was always in the second car, while we... me and KD... Kendra rode in the lead car. The other car would always be behind us. Once the money was counted and everything was good, whoever was buying the weed would get it from the second car. In this situation, Kendra and I was in my CTV-S coupe. I was driving and Kendra was in the passenger seat. Our friend Marshay was behind us in Kendra's Jaguar SUV. The twenty pounds were

134

in the SUV with Shay. The dude in all black runs up and shoots into the car. Kendra got hit—"

"Okay. First of all, you gotta be consistent, Daychelle. The grand jury is going to ask you questions after you testify. Your story cannot waver. When you and I first talked the day Ian introduced us, you said that Andy told y'all his cousin's name was Quintez or Quintay, but his nickname was Que. Remember that?"

Daychelle appeared to be in thought for a moment, then she spoke. "You're right. It was Andy who told us his cousin's name was Quintay."

"Good. Now remember what I said about good lies and bad lies?"

"I remember."

"When we first talked, you said that you couldn't tell who that person was that ran up on the car and shot Kendra. Remember that?"

"I remember that I said that, yeah."

"Okay. Let me say this. Later that day you saw an array of photos and you ID'd one of the photos as the man introduced to you as Andy's cousin. Remember that?"

Daychelle nodded.

"The man you met at your friend's house, the one that Andy introduced to you, was really a man named Quran Bashir. Let me ask you this, what reason do you think Andy and the man had to lie about Que's real name?"

"I don't know. Dudes give up fake names—"

"Don't get too bright on me, Daychelle. Just follow where I'm going with this. Quran Bashir is a killer. A paid killer. He didn't take any of the drugs or even attempt to. He didn't want weed. He wanted to kill Kendra Dyson. He was paid to kill her. Just like he was paid to kill Joseph Morris. You wanna know why?"

"Why?"

"Because Quran Bashir kills people who snitch. He's paid to kill people who testify against people. Joseph, 'JoJo' Morris was a snitch, Daychelle. Kendra was also a snitch—"

"I'm a snitch, too. He's going to kill me, right?"

"No, he's not. Why? Because he's going to be in jail. Once you go in that room and talk to those people in there, Quran goes to jail. I promise you that. All you have to do is say that you saw the guy who shot Kendra and that it was Que. I'll take care of the rest. So, let me ask you one more time. Did you recognize the person who shot Kendra at the bus depot and what did you know him as?" Daychelle Spencer got quiet. "If I go in there and say what you just said, that will get Que indicted, but it won't get him convicted unless I appear in court and take the stand and repeat my story. If I do that, I'm a marked woman for sure. If Que doesn't kill me, his friends will. So, I'm gonna tell that grand jury that I don't know no Que and that I never saw who killed Kendra. I want justice for Kendra, but I don't want to end up like she did. I'm a closet snitch, not one that's out in the open. I'd rather stay unknown. Thanks, but no thanks, Mr. Gamble. I don't know who killed JoJo or who killed Kendra."

* * *

If I was a tea kettle, this would be the part where the steam would be blowing out of my top. I walked around inside my office, livid at how my carefully laid plan had unraveled.

"You said too much, big mouth." My inner voice said. "You should have never told her that Quran Bashir was a Killer. Let alone a paid killer who killed rats. That spooked her."

Agreeing with my inner voice, all I could do was shake my head. Me and my big mouth. As I thought about how I was going to be able to get revenge against Quran Bashir, another thought hit. Something that I had heard, recently.

"*Later that day, Doo Doo said that two dudes came to the house. Sean Branch and a dude Sean called Quran Sean Branch killed Crud and cut his head off. The other dude with him killed Whistle—*"

"The other dude… the one that Sean called Quran killed Whistle?"

"*Yeah. Doo Doo said that Sean and the dude Quran said that Whistle was hot, too. That he had snitched on the same case. The one from MLK—*"

Picking up the phone, I made a call.

"Hello? Greg?" Tabitha Kearney answered.

"Tabitha, where are you?" I asked.

"I'm at District Court."

"In between cases?"

"In between appearances, yes."

"I know you're busy, but do you think you can arrange to have Joshua Clark to be brought here to talk to me?"

"When? Today?"

"Today. Tomorrow. Soon, though."

"I'll take care of it, Greg. I heard that you—"

Disconnecting the call, I made another. After a few rings, Detective Bob Mathis picked up.

"Bob, I need to question a guy. I need you to pick him up."

"Arrest him?" Bob Mathis asked.

"No. Just bring him in for questioning in a recent homicide."

"What homicide, Greg?"

"Joseph 'JoJo' Morris' homicide."

"And who is the person you want picked up?"

"Scambino. The notorious Andrew 'Scambino' Daniels. From Sursum Cordas."

* * *

Donovan Olsen was ex-CIA and Special Forces in Iraq in the early nineties during Desert Storm. Now, he was one of the best private investigators in the nation. Donovan she his

137

jacket and sat in the chair opposite my desk. To me he resembled Ben Affleck with a different color hair and hairstyle. Donovan opened a file and began to read.

"You already had a file on Paul Danielson. I dug a little more and basically came up with more of the same of what you have already. He's married but steps out on the wife often. Two kids, Benjamin and Maci, both attend different colleges on the West Coast. Danielson is a piece of shit as you know. Drugs... hard drugs, liquor, kinky sex, prostitutes, male escorts, Asian men and women in local massage parlors. Loves transgender women... or men, whichever is preferable. Known to take bribes. All from unsavory characters to avoid prosecution... mob bosses in Connecticut, Philly, and New Jersey. Owns a home in Martha's Vineyard where he parties every few months with elite, clandestine guest list. Has several offshore accounts in the Caymans and in the British Virgin Islands. Thinks he's slick as fish grease, Greg, but his efforts are all amateurish.

"Next up is Stephen Ross, heads the Justice Department, but he's also a piece of work. He was appointed to his position at Justice by Barack Obama in 2009. He praised President Obama in public, but secretly, he initiated the inquiries into Obama's citizenship and right to be President. Stephen Ross is former Klu Klux Klan—"

Donovan paused to hand me a set of photos. Glossy 6 x 9 shots of a young Stephen Ross in full KKK regalia. "It was hard getting those pics. Unearthing them took a lot of money, which I'm billing you for, by the way. After the Klan, he joined several right winged white supremacist groups... secretly, of course and silently indoctrinated those around him. He authored a paper in his freshman year of college at prestigious Yale that was rejected and buried by his professor and his parents. The title of that paper was, Apples and Black Men look best hanging from a Tree. Took a lot to get a cop of that paper, but I'm one of the best in the world at being persuasive...The intercom on my desk sounded.

IF YOU CROSS ME ONCE 6 | ANTHONY FIELDS

"Mr. Gamble, there are two people here to see you. Both say that you invited them."

"Send them in, please, Madelyn."

Donovan Olsen's eyes got as big as saucers. "You didn't tell me you were expecting company. I can come back at a later—"

"No, Don. Please continue. Your name is Dan Oliver. Remember it, please."

A knock at my office door made me stand and open the door. A man and a woman walked into my office with curious looks on their faces.

"This is Dan Oliver, an associate of mine. Dan, this lady here is Margerie Roth, and this gentleman is Sal Levin. Please, everyone, take a seat."

To be continued…

Lock Down Publications and Ca$h Presents
Assisted Publishing Packages

Due to an increase in the price of services we have increased our prices. The prices below reflect the price increase as of 11/1/24.

BASIC PACKAGE **$699** Editing Cover Design Formatting	UPGRADED PACKAGE **$1000** Typing Editing Cover Design Formatting Upload eBooks to Amazon Upload Paperback to Amazon
ADVANCE PACKAGE **$1,400** Typing Editing (line editing/content) Cover Design Formatting Copyright Registration Proofreading Upload eBooks to Amazon Upload Paperback to Amazon	LDP SUPREME PACKAGE **$1,700** Typing Editing (line editing/content) Cover Design Formatting Copyright Registration Proofreading Set up Amazon Account Upload eBooks to Amazon Upload Paperback to Amazon Advertise on LDP's Amazon and Facebook Page

***

Other services available upon request.
Additional charges may apply

Lock Down Publications
P.O. Box 944
Stockbridge, GA 30281-9998
Phone: 470 303-9761
Email: lockdownpublications@gmail.com

Submission Guideline

Submit the first three chapters of your completed manuscript to ldpsubmissions@gmail.com.In the subject line add **Your Book's Title**. The manuscript must be in a Word Doc file and sent as an attachment. Document should be in Times New Roman, double spaced, and in size 12 font. Also, provide your synopsis and full contact information. If sending multiple submissions, they must each be in a separate email.

Have a story but no way to send it electronically? You can still submit to LDP/Ca$h Presents. Send in the first three chapters, written or typed, of your completed manuscript to:

LDP: Submissions Dept
P.O. Box 944
Stockbridge, GA 30281-9998

DO NOT send original manuscript. Must be a duplicate.
Provide your synopsis and a cover letter containing your full contact information.

Thanks for considering LDP and Ca$h Presents.

NEW RELEASES

BLOODLINE OF A SAVAGE 1-3
THESE VICIOUS STREETS 1-3
RELENTLESS GOON 1-3
BY PRINCE A. TAUHID

THE BUTTERFLY MAFIA 1-3
BY FUMIYA PAYNE

A THUG'S STREET PRINCESS 1&2
BY MEESHA

CITY OF SMOKE 3
BY MOLOTTI

GET IT IN SLUGS 1 &2
BY B. STALL

STANDING ON HER BUSINESS 1&2
BY DG SANTANA

STEPPERS 1,2&3
THE REAL BADDIES OF CHI-RAQ
BY KING RIO

THE LANE 1&2
BY KEN-KEN SPENCE

THUG OF SPADES 1&2
LOVE IN THE TRENCHES 2
CORNER BOYS
BY COREY ROBINSON

TIL DEATH 3
BY ARYANNA

THE BIRTH OF A GANGSTER 4
BY DELMONT PLAYER

PRODUCT OF THE STREETS 1-3
BY DEMOND "MONEY" ANDERSON

NO TIME FOR ERROR
BY KEESE

MONEY HUNGRY DEMONS 1-2
BY TRANAY ADAMS

HUB CITY MENACE 1-3
BY J. WHITE

A THUGGISH PASSION 1&2
LAND OF DA HOOLIGANZ 1-4
KILLAZ ON STANDBY 1&2
BY IRA B.

FO'EVA ROLLIN 1&2
BY ASSA RAYMOND BAKER

THE LEVEL UP 1&3
BY LUXURY KING

Coming Soon from Lock Down Publications/Ca$h Presents

IF YOU CROSS ME ONCE 6
ANGEL V
By Anthony Fields

A THUGS STREET PRINCESS 3
By Meesha

CORNER BOYS 2
By Corey Robinson

THA TAKEOVER
By Keith Chandler

BETRAYAL OF A G 2
By Ray Vinci

SAVAGE FAMILY EMPIRE 1&2
SOULLESS GOON 1,2&3
THE DIRTY SIDE OF MONEY 1,2&3
By Prince

FOR MY ENEMY'S SAKE
AMBITIONS OF A SLIDER
FRESH OFF DA PORCH
By IRA B.

THE TRUCKLOAD 1-4
TIPPIN' THE SCALES 1-3
BAD BITCHES WIT GUNZ 3
PROBLEM SOLVED 2
By Christopher "Diesel" Hornezes

Available Now

RESTRAINING ORDER 1 & 2
By **CA$H & Coffee**

LOVE KNOWS NO BOUNDARIES 1-3
By **Coffee**

RAISED AS A GOON I, II, III & IV
BRED BY THE SLUMS I, II, III
BLAST FOR ME I & II
ROTTEN TO THE CORE I II III
A BRONX TALE I, II, III
DUFFLE BAG CARTEL I II III IV V VI
HEARTLESS GOON I II III IV V
A SAVAGE DOPEBOY I II
DRUG LORDS I II III
CUTTHROAT MAFIA I II
KING OF THE TRENCHES
By **Ghost**

LAY IT DOWN I & II
LAST OF A DYING BREED I II
BLOOD STAINS OF A SHOTTA I & II III
By **Jamaica**

LOYAL TO THE GAME I II III
LIFE OF SIN I, II III
By **TJ & Jelissa**

IF LOVING HIM IS WRONG…I & II
LOVE ME EVEN WHEN IT HURTS I II III
By **Jelissa**

PUSH IT TO THE LIMIT
By **Bre' Hayes**

145

BLOODY COMMAS I & II
SKI MASK CARTEL I, II & III
KING OF NEW YORK I II, III IV V
RISE TO POWER I II III
COKE KINGS I II III IV V
BORN HEARTLESS I II III IV
KING OF THE TRAP I II
By **T.J. Edwards**

WHEN THE STREETS CLAP BACK I & II III
THE HEART OF A SAVAGE I II III IV
MONEY MAFIA I II
LOYAL TO THE SOIL I II III
By **Jibril Williams**

A DISTINGUISHED THUG STOLE MY HEART I II & III
LOVE SHOULDN'T HURT I II III IV
RENEGADE BOYS 1-4
PAID IN KARMA 1-3
SAVAGE STORMS 1-3
AN UNFORESEEN LOVE 1-3
BABY, I'M WINTERTIME COLD 1-3
A THUG'S STREET PRINCESS 1&2
By **Meesha**

A GANGSTER'S CODE 1-3
A GANGSTER'S SYN 1-3
THE SAVAGE LIFE 1-3
CHAINED TO THE STREETS 1-3
BLOOD ON THE MONEY 1-3
A GANGSTA'S PAIN 1-3
BEAUTIFUL LIES AND UGLY TRUTHS
CHURCH IN THESE STREETS
By **J-Blunt**

CUM FOR ME 1-8
An LDP Erotica Collaboration

BLOOD OF A BOSS 1-5
SHADOWS OF THE GAME
TRAP BASTARD
By **Askari**

THE STREETS BLEED MURDER 1-3
THE HEART OF A GANGSTA 1-3
By **Jerry Jackson**

WHEN A GOOD GIRL GOES BAD
By **Adrienne**

THE COST OF LOYALTY 1-3
By **Kweli**

BRIDE OF A HUSTLA 1-3
THE FETTI GIRLS 1-3
CORRUPTED BY A GANGSTA 1-4
BLINDED BY HIS LOVE
THE PRICE YOU PAY FOR LOVE 1-3
DOPE GIRL MAGIC 1-3
By **Destiny Skai**

A KINGPIN'S AMBITION
A KINGPIN'S AMBITION II
I MURDER FOR THE DOUGH
By **Ambitious**

TRUE SAVAGE 1-7
DOPE BOY MAGIC 1-3
MIDNIGHT CARTEL 1-3
CITY OF KINGZ 1&2
NIGHTMARE ON SILENT AVE
THE PLUG OF LIL MEXICO 1&2
CLASSIC CITY
By **Chris Green**

A GANGSTER'S REVENGE 1-4
THE BOSS MAN'S DAUGHTERS 1-5
A SAVAGE LOVE1&2
BAE BELONGS TO ME 1&2
A HUSTLER'S DECEIT 1-3
WHAT BAD BITCHES DO 1-3
SOUL OF A MONSTER 1-3
KILL ZONE
A DOPE BOY'S QUEEN 1-3
TIL DEATH 1-3
IMMA DIE BOUT MINE 1-6
DYING FOR LIKES
By **Aryanna**

A DOPEBOY'S PRAYER
By **Eddie "Wolf" Lee**

THE KING CARTEL 1-3
By **Frank Gresham**

THESE NIGGAS AIN'T LOYAL 1-3
By **Nikki Tee**

GANGSTA SHYT 1-3
By **CATO**

THE ULTIMATE BETRAYAL
By **Phoenix**

BOSS'N UP 1-3
By **Royal Nicole**

I LOVE YOU TO DEATH
By **Destiny J**

I RIDE FOR MY HITTA
I STILL RIDE FOR MY HITTA
By **Misty Holt**

LOVE & CHASIN' PAPER
By **Qay Crockett**

TO DIE IN VAIN
SINS OF A HUSTLA
By **ASAD**

BROOKLYN HUSTLAZ
By **Boogsy Morina**

BROOKLYN ON LOCK 1 & 2
By **Sonovia**

GANGSTA CITY
By **Teddy Duke**

A DRUG KING AND HIS DIAMOND 1-3
A DOPEMAN'S RICHES
HER MAN, MINE'S TOO 1&2
CASH MONEY HO'S
THE WIFEY I USED TO BE 1&2
PRETTY GIRLS DO NASTY THINGS
By **Nicole Goosby**

LIPSTICK KILLAH 1-3
CRIME OF PASSION 1-3
FRIEND OR FOE 1-3
By **Mimi**

TRAPHOUSE KING 1-3
KINGPIN KILLAZ 1-3
STREET KINGS 1&2
PAID IN BLOOD 1&2
CARTEL KILLAZ 1-3
DOPE GODS 1&2
By **Hood Rich**

THE STREETS ARE CALLING
By **Duquie Wilson**

STEADY MOBBN' 1-3
THE STREETS STAINED MY SOUL 1-3
By **Marcellus Allen**

WHO SHOT YA 1-3
SON OF A DOPE FIEND 1-4
HEAVEN GOT A GHETTO 1&2
SKI MASK MONEY 1&2
By **Renta**

GORILLAZ IN THE BAY 1-4
TEARS OF A GANGSTA 1/&2
3X KRAZY 1&2
STRAIGHT BEAST MODE 1&2
By **DE'KARI**

TRIGGADALE 1-3
MURDA WAS THE CASE 1-3
By **Elijah R. Freeman**

SLAUGHTER GANG 1-3
RUTHLESS HEART 1-3
By **Willie Slaughter**

GOD BLESS THE TRAPPERS 1-3
THESE SCANDALOUS STREETS 1-3
FEAR MY GANGSTA 1-5
THESE STREETS DON'T LOVE NOBODY 1-2
BURY ME A G 1-5
A GANGSTA'S EMPIRE 1-4
THE DOPEMAN'S BODYGAURD 1&2
THE REALEST KILLAZ 1-3
THE LAST OF THE OGS 1-3
By **Tranay Adams**

MARRIED TO A BOSS 1-3
By **Destiny Skai & Chris Green**

KINGZ OF THE GAME 1-7
CRIME BOSS 1-4
By **Playa Ray**

FUK SHYT
By **Blakk Diamond**

DON'T F#CK WITH MY HEART 1&2
By **Linnea**

ADDICTED TO THE DRAMA 1-3
IN THE ARM OF HIS BOSS
By **Jamila**

LOYALTY AIN'T PROMISED 1&2
By **Keith Williams**

YAYO 1-4
A SHOOTER'S AMBITION 1&2
BRED IN THE GAME
By **S. Allen**

TRAP GOD1-3
RICH $AVAGE 1-3
MONEY IN THE GRAVE 1-3
CARTEL MONEY 1&2
By **Martell Troublesome Bolden**

FOREVER GANGSTA 1&2
GLOCKS ON SATIN SHEETS 1&2
By **Adrian Dulan**

TOE TAGZ 1-4
LEVELS TO THIS SHYT 1&2
IT'S JUST ME AND YOU
By **Ah'Million**

KINGPIN DREAMS 1-3
RAN OFF ON DA PLUG
By **Paper Boi Rari**

THE STREETS MADE ME 1-3
By **Larry D. Wright**

CONFESSIONS OF A GANGSTA 1-4
CONFESSIONS OF A JACKBOY 1-3
CONFESSIONS OF A HITMAN
CONFESSIONS OF A DOPE BOY
By **Nicholas Lock**

I'M NOTHING WITHOUT HIS LOVE
SINS OF A THUG
TO THE THUG I LOVED BEFORE
A GANGSTA SAVED XMAS
IN A HUSTLER I TRUST
By **Monet Dragun**

QUIET MONEY 1-3
THUG LIFE 1-3
EXTENDED CLIP 1&2
A GANGSTA'S PARADISE
By **Trai'Quan**

CAUGHT UP IN THE LIFE 1-3
THE STREETS NEVER LET GO 1-3
By **Robert Baptiste**

NEW TO THE GAME 1-3
MONEY, MURDER & MEMORIES 1-3
By **Malik D. Rice**

CREAM 2-3
THE STREETS WILL TALK
By **Yolanda Moore**

THE STREETS WILL NEVER CLOSE 1-3
By **K'ajji**

LIFE OF A SAVAGE 1-4
A GANGSTA'S QUR'AN 1-4
MURDA SEASON 1-3
GANGLAND CARTEL 1-3
CHI'RAQ GANGSTAS 1-4
KILLERS ON ELM STREET 1-3
JACK BOYZ N DA BRONX 1-3
A DOPEBOY'S DREAM 1-3
JACK BOYS VS DOPE BOYS 1-3
COKE GIRLZ
COKE BOYS
SOSA GANG 1&2
BRONX SAVAGES
BODYMORE KINGPINS
BLOOD OF A GOON
By **Romell Tukes**

CONCRETE KILLA 1-3
VICIOUS LOYALTY 1-3
BLOODY MONEY BAGS
By **Kingpen**

THE ULTIMATE SACRIFICE 1-6
KHADIFI
IF YOU CROSS ME ONCE 1-3
ANGEL 1-4
IN THE BLINK OF AN EYE
By **Anthony Fields**

THE LIFE OF A HOOD STAR
By **Ca$h & Rashia Wilson**

NIGHTMARES OF A HUSTLA 1-3
BLOOD AND GAMES 1&2
By **King Dream**

GHOST MOB
By **Stilloan Robinson**

HARD AND RUTHLESS 1&2
MOB TOWN 251
THE BILLIONAIRE BENTLEYS 1-3
REAL G'S MOVE IN SILENCE
By **Von Diesel**

MOB TIES 1-7
SOUL OF A HUSTLER, HEART OF A KILLER 1-3
GORILLAZ IN THE TRENCHES
OOPS CRY TOO 1&2
THE DAUGHTER OF A CARTEL BOSS
By **SayNoMore**

BODYMORE MURDERLAND 1-3
THE BIRTH OF A GANGSTER 1-4
By **Delmont Player**

FOR THE LOVE OF A BOSS 1&2
By **C. D. Blue**

KILLA KOUNTY 1-5
TENDER
By **Khufu**

MOBBED UP 1-4
THE BRICK MAN 1-5
THE COCAINE PRINCESS 1-10
STEPPERS 1-3
SUPER GREMLIN 1-4
A GANGSTA'S SON
By **King Rio**

MONEY GAME 1&2
By **Smoove Dolla**

A GANGSTA'S KARMA 1-5
By **FLAME**

KING OF THE TRENCHES 1-3
By **GHOST & TRANAY ADAMS**

BAD BITCHES WIT GUNZ 1&2
PROBLEM SOLVED
By "Christopher Diesel" Hornezes

QUEEN OF THE ZOO 1&2
By **Black Migo**

GRIMEY WAYS 1-3
BETRAYAL OF A G
By **Ray Vinci**

XMAS WITH AN ATL SHOOTER
By **Ca$h & Destiny Skai**

KING KILLA 1&2
By **Vincent "Vitto" Holloway**

BETRAYAL OF A THUG 1&2
By **Fre$h**

COUNTDOWN OF A KILLA 1&2
SEX, MURDER AND GOD 1&2
GUNS DOWN, BOTTOMS UP 1&2
By Lo-Life

THE MURDER QUEENS 1-7
By **Michael Gallon**

FOR THE LOVE OF BLOOD 1-4
By **Jamel Mitchell**

IF YOU CROSS ME ONCE 6 | ANTHONY FIELDS

HOOD CONSIGLIERE 1&2
NO TIME FOR ERROR
By **Keese**

PROTÉGÉ OF A LEGEND 1,2&3
LOVE IN THE TRENCHES 1&2
By **Corey Robinson**

THE PLUG'S RUTHLESS DAUGHTER 1&2
By **Tony Daniels**

BORN IN THE GRAVE 1-3
CRIME PAYS
By **Self Made Tay**

MOAN IN MY MOUTH
By **XTASY**

TORN BETWEEN A GANGSTER AND A GENTLEMAN
By **J-BLUNT & Miss Kim**

LOYALTY IS EVERYTHING 1-3
CITY OF SMOKE 1-3
By **Molotti**

HERE TODAY GONE TOMORROW 1&2
By **Fly Rock**

WOMEN LIE MEN LIE 1-4
FIFTY SHADES OF SNOW 1-3
STACK BEFORE YOU SPLURGE
GIRLS FALL LIKE DOMINOES
NAÏVE TO THE STREETS
By **ROY MILLIGAN**

PILLOW PRINCESS
By **S. Hawkins**

THE BUTTERFLY MAFIA 1-3
SALUTE MY SAVAGERY 1&2
By **Fumiya Payne**

THE LANE 1&2
By Ken-Ken Spence

THE PUSSY TRAP 1-5
By **Nene Capri**

DIRTY DNA
By **Blaque**

SANCTIFIED AND HORNY
by **XTASY**

BOOKS BY LDP'S CEO, CA$H

TRUST IN NO MAN
TRUST IN NO MAN 2
TRUST IN NO MAN 3
BONDED BY BLOOD
SHORTY GOT A THUG
THUGS CRY
THUGS CRY 2
THUGS CRY 3
TRUST NO BITCH
TRUST NO BITCH 2
TRUST NO BITCH 3
TIL MY CASKET DROPS
RESTRAINING ORDER
RESTRAINING ORDER 2
IN LOVE WITH A CONVICT
LIFE OF A HOOD STAR
XMAS WITH AN ATL SHOOTER